HARVEST OF DESPERATION

SAI SHRUTHI

Contents

Contents

I

Joseph

The last bell of the day, a cheerful, insistent ring, echoes through the brightly coloured hallways of Elmwood Elementary, signalling the end of another whirlwind afternoon. "Alright, my little adventurers!" My voice, warm and melodic, carries easily over the excited chatter of twenty small voices, a familiar symphony of youthful exuberance. "That's all for today! Hope you enjoyed the story about the brave little squirrel who found the biggest acorn in the forest."

A chorus of "Yes, Mr. Garry!" erupts, their enthusiasm undimmed by the prospect of dismissal. A few children, still captivated by the lingering magic of the tale, cluster by my desk, their eyes wide with wonder, tiny hands gripping the edges of my worn wooden surface.

"Mr. Garry, will you tell us another story on Monday?" asks Anna, her pigtails bouncing with her eager movements as she leans forward, her face alight with curiosity. Her eyes, usually so observant, are now solely focused on the promise of continuation.

I chuckle, a soft, rumbling sound that always seems to put them at ease, and I kneel down, bringing myself to her level. "Of course, Anna. Every Monday, we'll dive into a new adventure. Until then, have a happy weekend. Now, off you go, your parents are waiting! Don't keep them worrying."

I watch them go, a genuine smile spreading across my face as they bounce out the door, a scattering of bright colours and joyful shrieks. The classroom, usually filled with energy and noise, settles into a quiet calm, the lingering scent of crayons and construction paper a comforting embrace. I love this part of the day, the gentle winding down, the lingering echoes of young minds engaged, curious, and utterly delighted. Teaching isn't just a job for me; it's a calling, a profound source of quiet joy that fills a space deep within my chest. I find immense satisfaction in seeing the spark of understanding ignite in a child's eyes, the way their imaginations take flight with a simple story, soaring beyond the classroom walls. I move around the room, tidying up stray crayons and picture books, gently aligning stacks of worksheets, my movements unhurried, a sense of deep contentment settling over me like a warm blanket.

The late afternoon sun slants through the large classroom windows, painting long, golden rectangles on the worn wooden floor, illuminating dust motes dancing in the air like tiny, forgotten stars. I stretch, a comfortable sigh escaping my lips, the kind that comes from a day well spent. "Another good day," I murmur to the empty room. I gather my satchel, a familiar weight on my shoulder, and lock the classroom door behind me, the click echoing softly in the now silent hall.

The walk home is a familiar, comforting routine, a gentle transition from the structured chaos of the school day to the quiet rhythm of my own personal life. The air is crisp, carrying the faint scent of freshly cut grass from someone's manicured lawn and the sweet, heady bloom of lilacs from a nearby bush, a symphony of simple, natural fragrances. I stop at the small grocery store on the corner. The bell above the door jingles cheerfully as I enter, announcing my arrival.

"Evening, Mr. Garry!" Maria, the owner, greets me from behind the counter, with a warm smile that crinkles the corners of her eyes.

"Evening, Maria," I reply, returning her smile. I pick up a carton of milk, a loaf of crusty bread, and a few ripe apples, their skins gleaming red under the store's soft lights. With my canvas bag filled, I pay, exchange a few more pleasantries about the day's pleasant weather, and step back out into the fading light, heading towards the familiar, welcoming comfort of my own small home.

The aroma of my simple dinner—a hastily prepared omelette and the crusty bread I'd just bought—fills my small kitchen as I eat, the quiet hum of the refrigerator my only company. It's a peaceful solitude, a welcome change from the energetic buzz of the classroom. After cleaning up, I settle onto my worn armchair in the living room, a book open on my lap. But my gaze keeps drifting to the empty space on the rug beside me.

A soft thump from the bedroom startles me, followed by a low, rumbling meow. Mr. Whiskers, my beloved orange tabby, has clearly finished his own meal and is now ready for his evening ritual. He hops onto the bed and then, with surprising agility for his rotund frame, gracefully jumps onto the armchair next to me, meowing again, a soft, insistent sound that is impossible to ignore. I snap out of my thoughts, the lingering echoes of the day fading as I turn my full attention to him. He slowly blinks his large, golden eyes at me, a gesture of profound trust and affection that always melts any lingering stress. I reciprocate, slowly blinking back, a silent conversation between us, and then gently boop his tiny, velvet nose with my finger. He meows again, a satisfied rumble vibrating through his chest, and then, with a determined push, nuzzles against me, burrowing into my side, kneading my shirt with his soft paws. And that's when I realize, with a quiet certainty that settles deep in my chest, a warmth radiating from my core, that his simple, unconditional affection is a profound comfort.

The next morning, Sunday Sun makes its view clear from my window, bathing my room in a soft, golden light. I wake to the soft weight of Mr. Whiskers snuggling against my side, a warm, purring bundle in his sleep. His rhythmic purr is a gentle vibration against my ribs, a soothing lullaby. I pet him, his fur incredibly soft beneath my fingers, as he sleeps like a baby, utterly trusting, completely oblivious to the world outside his dreams. I spend a few more moments simply enjoying his presence, the quiet comfort he brings. Then, with a reluctant sigh, I carefully ease myself out of bed, careful not to disturb him, and make my way to freshen up, the routine a familiar anchor, grounding me in the present.

After a leisurely breakfast, I head out for a walk, enjoying the quiet calm of a Sunday morning in my little village. As I wander, letting my feet lead me, a small, unassuming coffee shop catches my eye, its windows steaming faintly. A coffee to go, perhaps, a nice little treat for a quiet day. When I enter, the rich aroma of roasted beans envelops me, a comforting cloud. A couple sits intimately in a sunlit corner, their hands clasped, their eyes lost in each other, while a boisterous group of young men occupies the opposite side of the shop, their laughter echoing cheerfully. I am near the counter when a young lady, her shoulders slumped, her posture radiating a profound sadness, orders a latte. The waitress asks for her name, and she replies, "Megan," in a voice so soft it's barely a whisper, thick with unspoken sorrow. She takes a seat near the window, her back to the room, facing the street. And suddenly, my impulse to simply grab a coffee and leave vanishes. I decide to stay. I order a Frappuccino, the chilly sweetness a contrast to the heavy atmosphere I sense. I choose the seat directly behind her, so we are back-to-back, a silent, unacknowledged proximity.

She's on the phone, her voice low and strained, punctuated by choked sobs that pierce the murmur of the coffee shop. "I am done," she whispers, the words raw with despair, tearing at the fabric of my own calm. "I can't take this anymore. I wanna end it."

At that, I take a slow sip of my coffee, the cold sweetness barely registering. Then, with a deliberate slowness that feels both natural and entirely planned, I rise and sit across from her. Her eyes, wide and tear-filled, meet mine in a strange, startled look before she quickly hangs up, her hand trembling. I pull a clean handkerchief from my pocket and extend it to her, gesturing subtly to her tear-streaked face. She hesitates for a moment, her gaze searching mine, then takes it, pressing it to her eyes, wiping away the fresh tears.

"You can keep it," I tell her, my voice gentle, almost sympathetic, meant to convey understanding rather than pity. She offers me a weak, half-smile, a flicker of something in her eyes. "You're right, by the way," I continue, my gaze unwavering, holding hers. "You should end whatever it is that makes you feel like this." I rise from the table, leaving her with her thoughts, the weight of my words hanging in the air, and turn to leave the coffee shop.

If I am right, she will follow me outside. Five steps away from the coffee shop, just as the jingle of the bell fades behind me, I hear her call, "Hey!" I halt, a subtle, knowing smile playing on my lips. She is definitely the right person.

When I turn, she is right in front of me, her eyes still red-rimmed but now alight with a fierce, desperate curiosity, a spark of life returning.

"What did you mean by that?" she demands, her voice trembling, but stronger than before.

"I meant," I move close to her ear, my voice dropping to a low, almost conspiratorial whisper, "*End it.*"

II
Daniel

"Babe, I think I may be late tonight. These cases are... time-consuming, with no actual leads." The words feel heavy on my tongue, a familiar, bitter refrain. I hear her sigh on the other side of the phone, a soft, weary exhalation that twists a knot of guilt in my stomach. It has been weeks, perhaps months, since I've been able to spend quality time with Jessica, not since these 'missing cases' began their relentless, baffling march. And she hasn't been herself lately, a quiet melancholy clinging to her like a shroud, dimming the vibrant spark I love. We've been married for five years now, and in so many ways, I couldn't be happier with my life. Yet, something feels empty, a hollow space within our shared existence. It's probably the children. Or rather, the lack of them. The *can't* rather than the *don't*.

Jessica loves kids with a fierce, aching tenderness, and it tears me apart that she can't have one of her own. I've been trying, endlessly, to make her feel better, to suggest other options—adoption, surrogacy, anything—but she can't bear the raw, inescapable fact that she won't be able to experience motherhood in the way she dreams.

"I know, babe. Listen, I will make it up to you tomorrow. I swear." I wait, the silence stretching for a few agonizing seconds, punctuated only by the distant hum of the precinct office. Then, her voice, small and fragile, finally breaks it. "You promise?" I breathe out a sigh of relief, a silent, grateful puff of air, and a small, genuine smile touches my lips. "Of course. I am so sorry for today, though."

"No, don't be," she replies, her voice a little stronger now, a hint of her usual resilience returning. "It's your job, I get it. I just feel like we haven't been able to do stuff together, you know?"

"I know, I do," I echo, the words heavy with genuine regret. "I feel terrible, but hey, no matter what, tomorrow, I am all yours. Whatever you need. Okay?" I say, my voice tinged with a pleading tone, a desperate hope that she will believe me, that I can somehow make it right. I can't see her, but I imagine her smiling on the other end, a faint, wistful curve of her lips, when she finally says, "Alrighty, Detective. Get back to work. Bye." At least, that's what I tell myself, I think, the familiar self-deception a bitter taste on my tongue. I hang up, the click of the receiver final, and turn back to the stack of files on my desk. I've been assigned this case, this relentless string of disappearances, because it is a continual crime, possibly orchestrated by the same phantom.

"The victim's wife is here, Dan," Officer Bell says, his voice low, pulling me from the cold labyrinth of case files. I nod, the movement stiff, and follow him down the sterile hallway. The air in the precinct always carries a faint, metallic tang of stale coffee and unspoken anxieties. We stop outside the interview room, the frosted glass offering no comfort. My gaze falls upon her, the woman seated within. Her face is a swollen landscape of grief, all red and puffed up from endless crying, her eyes raw and vacant, staring at some unseen horror. This is the part I hate the most. Not because I dread talking to them, the families left behind in the wake of inexplicable absences. But because I don't exactly know how to talk to them, what to say, or what to do. My training has prepared me for facts, for evidence, for the cold logic of crime scenes, not for the crushing weight of human despair.

She looks at us, her gaze unfocused, then sharpens with a terrible certainty. "He is dead, isn't he?"

And there it is. The question that hangs in the air like a death knell, a question I can't answer. Because I don't know! Not about him, not about the other missing people. The helplessness is a suffocating cloak, tightening around my throat.

"I really hope he isn't," I manage, the words feeling utterly inadequate, a flimsy attempt to console her.

"It's been over a week now!" she cries, her voice cracking, and fresh tears stream down her face, carving paths through the dried salt on her cheeks. It breaks my heart, this raw, unbridled agony. I hate that I can't do anything, that my hands are tied by the invisible threads of this baffling case. Before I can even formulate another platitude, she drops to the floor, a crumpled heap of despair, her sobs echoing in the small, silent room. "Just tell me he is gone," she wails, her voice a desperate plea, "The least you can do is help me find closure!"

"Miss, I am truly sorry that you are going through this, but we are doing the best we can," Officer Bell says, his voice surprisingly gentle, a stark contrast to his usual gruff demeanor. He kneels, his hand steady on her arm, helping her to her feet. "I know what I am saying sounds like an excuse. The truth is that we are afraid of the possibility of him being dead as well. The others who went missing before your husband haven't been found. We think they might have passed away. But since your husband is the last person to go missing, we are still holding onto the hope that he might be alive."

"Or maybe," I add, stepping forward, my voice low and earnest, "all of them are alive somewhere and they were just abducted for some reason. We have no clue as to who is doing this or why." She wipes her tears with the back of her hand, lets out a huge, shuddering sigh that seems to empty her lungs, and then turns towards the door. She halts, her hand on the frame, her shoulders slumped, a figure of utter defeat. "He is not coming back, I know it. I can feel him gone!" And then she is gone, leaving behind only the lingering scent of her grief and the heavy silence of the room.

I just stand there, the silence pressing in, not knowing how to go about it, how to process the raw despair I've just witnessed. How much she must have been through, how deeply she must have suffered, to just give up hope like that, is something I can't begin to understand. There's no way to look for whatever we missed while investigating, because we've already found absolutely nothing. No pieces of evidence whatsoever. The day he went missing, his wife told us about his whereabouts and who he was with, but that lead dissolved into thin air, a phantom trail. Although, when we inquire about him to his colleagues, they mention that he isn't really in his right mind. That he always seems off and sad, withdrawn, almost as if a light has gone out inside him. But the chilling thing is, it isn't just him. The others who went missing are also in a similar phase as him, a shared tapestry of quiet desperation. It's the only common thread among all the missing people: they are all profoundly unhappy with their lives.

Maybe all of them just killed themselves. That thought, dark and unsettling, crosses my mind plenty of times, a grim possibility that offers a twisted kind of logic. But deep down, I know that it doesn't really make sense. Even if they are so utterly done with their lives to the point where they have to commit suicide, we might have found their bodies sooner or later. Or, they might have left traces somehow, a note, a sign, anything. And they wouldn't have gone missing one by one, in the name of suicide, without a single trace. It's all so confusing, so frustrating, and I am fed up with it. People are losing their lives, disappearing into thin air, and here we are, the supposed protectors, with absolutely no leads, whatsoever.

"I think this case is gonna be just as much of a pain in the ass as the last one," Officer Bell says, his voice flat, echoing my own unspoken thoughts. I nod in agreement, the weariness settling deeper into my bones. "How come we are not able to find them, Bell? I thought we were good at this. Isn't that why we do this as a profession? To find answers?"

"I have been thinking that ever since I joined the precinct, Dan. It'll pass. You'll see," Officer Bell says, matter-of-factly, his gaze distant, as if looking through the wall. He has a way of accepting the grim realities of the job that I envy, a kind of stoic resignation. I, on the other hand, do have regrets about choosing this profession. At first, I want to do this because I have a knack for crime-solving, a thrill in piecing together the puzzles, in bringing justice. But now, it's just another day, another missing person, another dead end. To do this as a profession, every single day, to face this relentless tide of human misery and baffling crimes, is ridiculous. I don't find it fun as I did before. Not only is it not progressive and worth it, but I haven't been able to balance my work and personal life. And these cases have piled up, a suffocating weight, precisely because we aren't able to crack them, to find the missing victims. It's like this case has no end, an endless, twisting labyrinth. And the person doing all of this is probably an omnipotent being with magical powers, a ghost in the machine. Or maybe just an average person who is really, terrifyingly good at what he does. Maybe it's a she. I can't even tell anymore.

This sucks. All I want is to find this person, this phantom, and end this for good.

If only it were easier to do.

III

Joseph

The sharp rap on my door makes me jump, pulling me instantly from the detailed lesson plan for Tuesday's class. When I open it, John stands there, a paper bag from the bakery in one hand, a wide, familiar grin on his face. "Garry! Look at you, living the dream," he teases, stepping past me into the cozy familiarity of my small living room. "Still crafting those macaroni necklaces and molding young minds, I see." He gestures vaguely around my living room, probably eyeing the stack of children's books on my coffee table.

I just shake my head, a fond smile spreading across my face. John, a brilliant cardiac surgeon and my college mate. Despite our wildly different academic paths, our bond remains strong. He's a successful surgeon, saving lives every day, and I, well, I'm a respected teacher, trying to shape lives.

"So, how's the 'doctor' life treating you? Saving every patient?" My question, though laced with sarcasm, holds genuine curiosity.

John sighs, the weight of his profession evident in his voice. "It's harder than you can imagine. Failing to save a patient... it makes you question everything, all the years of study, the sacrifices. It feels like it was all in vain." I empathize deeply, because we do share a common frustration: the preventable loss of life due to inefficient delivery systems.

"Speaking of which, how are you holding up?" John's question pulls me from my thoughts. "Well, you know, I'm living."

"I can see that," he says, concern etched on his face. "Don't tire yourself out too much. You look like you haven't slept in forever. Are you having trouble sleeping?"

"No, it's just... I really dedicate myself to making sure the kids have the best time possible in my class. Plus, I've had other things on my plate," I admit with a sigh. He nods understandingly. "Well, make time to take care of yourself." As he heads for the door, he pauses. "Stop by for a check-up or something." I give him a thumbs-up. "Will do."

Once he leaves, I go in search of Mr. Whiskers. I find him on my bed, meticulously grooming himself, his orange fur gleaming under the afternoon light. I hop on beside him. "I'm sorry I haven't been able to make time for you," I tell him, stroking his soft fur. "Shall we go out for some fresh air, perhaps?" He continues his meticulous cleaning, unfazed by my human babbling. I wait patiently until he's done, then scoop him up, a purring, contented weight in my arms. "We're going shopping , little man. Let's get you some food and accessories."

At the pet store, a world of toys, treats, and necessities unfolds before us. The air hums with the happy barks and chirps of various creatures, and many shoppers have brought their furry companions along, their leashes tangling in the aisles. I place Mr. Whiskers gently in the trolley, his large golden eyes surveying his temporary perch with an air of regal curiosity, and navigate the aisles, searching for his favorite salmon-flavored treats.

"Wow, that's such an adorable cat! What's her name?" two women gush, approaching me with bright, eager smiles.

I look up from the rack of catnip toys, offering them a small, polite smile. "Well, it's a he," I clarify, my voice even, "and his name is Mr. Whiskers." I give a slight nod, a subtle gesture of acknowledgment, and then, with a quiet apology, maneuver the trolley past them, gently cutting off any further conversation. I generally avoid strangers and their attempts at small talk; it's not rudeness, just a preference for my own quiet space. After selecting some special treats and a few crinkly toys I think Mr. Whiskers will enjoy, I join the checkout line, the trolley rumbling softly.

Mr. Whiskers, sensing an opportunity for adventure, begins to squirm in the trolley, his tail twitching with anticipation. I pick him up and set him on the polished floor, curious to see where his instincts will lead him. He quickly spots a towering cat tree house, a multi-tiered kingdom of scratching posts and cozy perches, and with an impressive, silent leap, lands inside the highest cubby. He settles in, looking utterly content and peaceful, his eyes half-closed in feline bliss. I know then, with a quiet certainty, that I have to buy it for him, along with a few small bells to hang around it, to keep him entertained for hours.

When we arrive home, the delivery van is already there, a large, white presence in front of my house. I direct the movers to carefully place the cat tree house in the living room, a space that suddenly feels less empty with its grand addition, and pay them, signing the delivery slip. As they are leaving, one of the men, a burly fellow with a friendly, if overly familiar, demeanour, remarks, "It's a great place you have here, sir. But you must be lonely living all alone in this huge house."

I turn to face him, a faint, polite smile still on my lips, though my eyes hold a firm, unspoken boundary. "My living arrangements are quite comfortable, thank you," I say, my voice even, leaving no room for further personal inquiry. I gesture subtly towards the front door. "The door is right there. Please show yourselves out." I don't wait for a reply, simply turn and head upstairs to my room, the soft thud of their retreating footsteps fading behind me. I collapse onto my bed, staring at the ceiling, the quiet of the house settling around me once more. A phone call interrupts my quiet, an unknown number flashing on the screen. I ignore it, placing my phone aside, and close my eyes, letting the day's events gently recede.

IV
Daniel

I wait in the living room, a vibrant bouquet of roses beside me, pretending to read a book, though my eyes keep darting to the bedroom door. Today, I have a series of fun activities planned, and I hope she'll be as excited as I am. The bedroom door finally opens, and she emerges, a vision in the blue dress she loves. It's the same dress she wore when I proposed, a dress she hasn't worn since our wedding day. This is a good sign, a ripple of hope unfurling in my chest.

"You look absolutely gorgeous," I say, rising to meet her, the words sincere. I hand her the roses, their scent filling the air, and she rewards me with a small, sweet smile, a shy warmth blooming in her eyes. A quick peck on her cheek leads to a warm embrace. We hold each other for nearly a minute, just breathing her in, before she gently pulls back. "We should get going. We're running late," she murmurs, a hint of anticipation in her voice.

I nod, leading her towards the front door. She pauses, turning to me, a faint worry clouding her expression. "Are you sure you can spend the whole day without being needed at the precinct? I mean, you don't have to do this if you're busy. I know the cases are piling up."

"I'm free today, and besides, I need a day off. I've been swamped with work lately. I'm sure the precinct can manage for a day without me. Today is all about having fun. Come on," I say, locking the door and taking her hand. I make sure to do everything exactly as I did on our first date: complimenting her, giving her flowers, holding her hand, and opening the car door for her. These gestures aren't new; I do them almost every time we're together. But she loves the small things, the little acts of devotion, and her smile is all the reward I need.

She gazes out the window, a soft smile playing on her lips. "Where are we going, by the way?" she asks, her voice light with curiosity. I glance at her, a knowing smile on my face. When she turns to look at me, I simply look ahead as I drive. "You'll see." I turn on the stereo, and "Love You Like a Love Song" by Selena Gomez fills the car, its catchy rhythm a perfect soundtrack for the day.

When we arrive, she doesn't recognize it at first. Then, after a few moments, her eyes light up with recognition and surprise. The book cafe, now a book and pet cafe. It's even better with animals around. She steps inside, her face alight with wonder. Dogs and cats play and snuggle in cozy corners, making the atmosphere even more inviting than before, a joyful hum filling the space. She wanders around, stopping to play with the pets, her laughter echoing through the space, light and free. She looks happier than she has in a long time, and a quiet relief washes over me. I find a corner seat near the window, the exact spot where I first saw her years ago, engrossed in a book, watching the world outside. She was so peaceful, so beautiful. It still amazes me that she agreed to go out with me, let alone marry me. It's a memory I cherish, a foundational moment in our story.

My gaze drifts to the wall beside the window. There, near the frame, is a small, faded doodle art with our names: "*Jesse♡Dan 4ever*," followed by a heart. I trace it with my finger, transported back to that beautiful moment, the beginning of everything.

A Few Years Ago...

I walk into the book cafe with my friend, Jack, looking for a cup of coffee, a quiet refuge from the bustle of the city. Then I see her. She's sitting in the corner, near the window, a cup of coffee in front of her, a book in her hand. She takes a sip, her eyes still on the page, completely absorbed. I'm staring, mesmerized, until Jack slaps the back of my head.

"Dude, you're being creepy, right?" he whispers, pulling me away from my trance. "Stop staring at her. You look like a weirdo."

I do the opposite, of course, but subtly, ensuring she can't see me. I'm not staring; I'm admiring. I silently and secretly admire her the entire time she reads, captivated by her quiet grace. As dusk settles, painting the sky in hues of orange and purple, she finally finishes her book. She walks in my direction, and I freeze, unable to move, my heart thumping against my ribs. She nears me, and just as I think I can finally strike up a conversation, she walks past, but not without a quick, curious glance in my direction, a fleeting acknowledgment. She walks out of the cafe, and that's when I realize I've consumed three cups of coffee and probably don't have enough money for them. Thankfully, Jack has nodded off in the corner, completely oblivious. I wake him up, and with a groan, he pays for the coffees.

"I can't believe we wasted our time here," he grumbles, rubbing his eyes. I try to cheer him up, persuading him to come back with me every day, hoping to run into her again. He resists at first, groaning about his wasted afternoon, but my desperation eventually wins him over. "But only if you man up and talk to her, Dan. Otherwise, this is just stalking, you understand?"

"Yeah, I got it. Thanks, bud," I say, nodding, already planning my opening line.

The next day, we return to the cafe, waiting for her to show up, a silent vigil. But she doesn't. Jack starts reading, while I sit there, lost in thought, my gaze fixed on the door. After a while, I order a coffee and move to the seat she had occupied the day before. I understand why she chose it. It offers a great window view, is close to the book rack, and provides a sense of quiet privacy. It's a perfect spot.

I wait for almost an hour and a half, nursing my coffee, but she never appears. Maybe she doesn't come here every day. I look for Jack, but he's engrossed in his book, so I leave him to it. When he finally finishes, he closes the book with a frustrated sigh, a clear sign of his annoyance. He approaches me. "So... she stood you up, huh?"

"What?" I laugh, a genuine, bewildered sound. "Dude, it's been like twenty-four hours since I saw her for the first time, and we haven't even met face to face yet. She doesn't know who I am. What are you talking about?" I laugh again, shaking my head.

"Exactly," he says firmly, his eyes unwavering. "Let's go." He walks out, leaving me there, feeling utterly foolish, a sense of defeat creeping in.

What am I even doing here? For a second, I rethink my decisions and almost give up. Almost.

The next day, I'm back, hoping against hope that she will show up. But no. She doesn't appear for the next five days either. Maybe that was her last visit to the cafe. Perhaps she didn't like it that much, or the books weren't good enough. Or maybe she lives too far away to come every day. Jack is furious and wants to distance himself from me for a while. It makes sense; I'm being ridiculous.

I'm almost convinced she won't come, that I've lost my chance, that this impossible quest is finally over. But something tells me she might show up today, and that's why I'm here again, for the last time, or so I tell myself. This time, I'm alone. Jack refused to be embarrassed again, and frankly, I don't blame him. I wait in the same spot I've occupied for the past six days, nursing a single cup of lukewarm coffee. A while later, the bell chimes as the door opens. I look up, anticipation surging through me, and then I'm smiling from ear to ear. She walks in, wearing a pretty blue jumpsuit, her hair tied in a messy bun. She looks even cuter than she did a week ago.

A week ago... that's right. Today is Saturday. She was here last Saturday. So, she comes here every Saturday. I've figured it out. And thank God I showed up today. My intuition was right.

She picks out a book and sits across from me, in her usual spot. She never once looks up, her focus entirely on her reading. I can't tell if it's intentional or if she simply doesn't care about my presence. But I don't mind. I just sit there, watching her read, memorizing the way her brow furrows in concentration, the curve of her smile when something in the book amuses her. She remains engrossed until she finishes the book, about an hour and a half later. Then, she goes to replace the book on the rack and leaves. The entire time, I've just watched her, seated in the same spot, too nervous to speak.

I stand up and walk out the front door, noticing her leaning against the wall outside, her phone in hand. Was she waiting for me? Before I can approach her, she speaks. "Were you waiting for me?"

She has stolen my line.

I don't respond immediately, taking a step forward, my mind racing for a witty reply. She turns away, "Guess not," and starts to walk.

"Yes!" I call out, my voice halting her. I can't take it back now. I squeeze my eyes shut in embarrassment, bracing for her reaction. "Yeah, I was waiting for you. For the past week, actually." She slowly turns to face me, a faint smile playing on her lips.

A witty smile plays on her lips. "Finally. I was waiting for you to admit it."

I look at her, astonished, my mouth slightly agape. She continues, enjoying my dumbfounded expression. "I've been watching you wait for me for the past week. The first day, I thought you were just passing time, being all goofy. But then I saw you the next day, sitting in the same spot, with an eager expression on your face. I didn't come in because I wanted to see what you'd do next. And then I saw you waiting for me every day. That was kind of cute. In fact, I came here just so I could see you waiting for me." She admits it with a mischievous grin, her eyes dancing.

"But I finally decided to come in today. I had to try so hard not to laugh or show any sign of my plan. However, you just kept staring at me. I was expecting you to start a conversation, but nada. That's why I thought of initiating it. So, were you just planning on staring at me the whole time?" I look at her, a questionable expression on my face, my mind reeling. I can't find the right words. I'm stunned.

She then says, "Fine. Wanna grab something to eat?" I still can't speak, perhaps because of her straightforwardness, or simply because she looks absolutely gorgeous, bathed in the soft afternoon light. When I don't answer, she turns away again, saying, "Guess not," and starts walking.

"Yes!" I yell again, louder this time, a desperate plea.

I possibly can't embarrass myself any more than this. But it is worth it.

She turns, a wide smile on her face, a radiant beam that lights up my entire world. "Let's go," she says, locking arms with me and leading me towards wherever she is taking me. And that's how we met. The rest is history.

Present Day...

Jessica waves a hand in front of my face, snapping me out of my reverie. "You still with me, Dan?"

I smile, reaching for her hand across the table. "Of course. How long has it been? Seven years? And I'm still with you. Always will be."

She lets out a small laugh, a soft, melodic sound. "You do realize you stare a lot, right?"

"Okay, first of all, that's the look of love. I only stare at beautiful things. That's you. And second of all, you know what they say: Old habits die hard." I shrug with a hint of a smile, a playful admission. Her eyes fall on the wall where the doodle art is drawn, a faint, nostalgic curve to her lips. She looks at it, then at me.

"You were so tacky back then," she says, a fond amusement in her voice. "And with all your doodling and stuff, you were childish and funny."

"Isn't that why you fell for me in the first place?" I ask playfully, a sarcastic smile on my face, already knowing the answer.

"Yeah, you would think, wouldn't you?" she chuckles, squeezing my hand. I reach across the table and hold her hand, interlacing our fingers. "I've got to be the luckiest guy in the world to have found the perfect woman that every guy wishes for. I love you, Jess."

She looks down, and I can't tell if she's blushing or shy, a private moment unfolding. "Jess?" I prompt, squeezing her hand gently. She looks up, a wide, genuine smile spreading across her face, her eyes shining. "I love you too, Dan." I release her hand and stand up. "Let me go get us a cup of coffee." She nods, turning to look out the window, back to the world of books and pets.

As I reach our table with the coffee cups, my phone rings, a jarring intrusion. I hand her her cup and place mine on the table before answering. My face tightens as I listen to the caller, the precinct's urgent tone already familiar. Jessica, perceptive as ever, catches my shift in demeanour. When I hang up, she offers a tight-lipped smile, understanding dawning in her eyes. "Duty calls, huh?" A wave of terrible guilt washes over me.

"Hey, you should go. I'll be fine. Besides, it's been so long since I've been here. I can read books all day. Sounds like a fun day for me. Trust me, I'll be okay. Go." She tries to assure me, her voice softening, but I remain silent, knowing she's just trying to make it easier for me, but feeling worse, nonetheless. I lean down and kiss her forehead, a lingering touch. "I'll be back before you finish a book. Wait for me." She smiles, a brave, wistful smile, and I leave her there, alone with her books and thoughts, the weight of the unsolved cases already pressing down on me.

At the precinct, Officer Bell approaches me, his expression grim. "The missing person is—"

I cut him off, my mind already racing, processing the implications. "Spare me the details. Where's her friend you mentioned?" He points to a young woman, huddled in a chair, and I walk over to question her. She stands as I near, her eyes wide with apprehension.

"You are—"

"Paige. Megan's friend," she interrupts, her voice trembling slightly.

I nod, asking her to sit and calm herself. She's visibly trembling with fear and nervousness, twisting her hands in her lap. "You're here just to answer a few questions since you were the last person to speak to her on the phone," I explain, my tone calm and reassuring.

After a moment, she begins to speak, her voice barely a whisper. "I did speak to her. She sounded more down than usual. She was always on the edge, talking about ending her life. That day, she was going on about how she didn't want to live and wanted it all to be over. I tried talking her out of it and consoling her, but—" She pauses, tears streaming down her face, her shoulders shaking with silent sobs. "What if... did she perhaps... kill herself?" she chokes out, her gaze pleading. I can't console her when I have no answers myself, the helplessness a familiar, bitter taste.

"That is exactly what we want to find out, Paige. And for that, we need your help." She nods, wiping her tears with the back of her hand, a flicker of resolve in her eyes.

After a thorough inquiry, taking in all the information we've received, trying to piece together what has happened, we release her. Like so many other missing persons cases, this one is almost a dead end. We have a name, a last conversation, and the chilling, familiar thread of despair.

"There has to be some kind of loophole or something," Officer Bell says, rubbing the back of his neck, his voice mirroring my own frustration. I nod in agreement, my mind racing, searching for any hint, any thread to pull in this tangled web of disappearances.

V

Joseph

"I don't think this is necessary," I say, handing the small bottle of pills back to John. My sleep schedule is so erratic lately, a chaotic dance between lesson planning and my own thoughts, I doubt any number of pills could truly fix it.

"You think you can keep living like this with everything you are doing, Joe?" John retorts, his voice laced with concern, his surgeon's eyes missing nothing. "The least you can do is take care of your eating and sleeping habits. You look like you're running on fumes."

"I hear you, John. You make it sound like I'm some heartbroken teenager sick and tired of life," I say, trying to lighten the mood as I stand up, grabbing my coat from the back of the chair. "Look, this is temporary. Once the school year winds down a bit, I'll be fine. I'll see you later, doc."

"Yeah, because the *school* is what's making you look like shit." He says.

I halt. "You need all the strength and health if you want to keep helping people," he adds. "Sometimes, even heroes need rest."

We both know what he means by that. He has been the major aid in making all the things happen. I wouldn't be able to do what I am doing if not him or his constant help.

I just give him a nod and head out of his cabin, the brisk air of the hospital corridor a welcome shock to my face. I take a deep breath, the faint antiseptic scents, a stark contrast to the lively chaos of Elmwood Elementary. The dimly lit corridor stretches before me, casting long shadows as I make my way towards the exit. A blast of cold air hits me as I push through the automatic doors, making me shiver slightly. The world outside buzzes with activity—chatter, footsteps echoing against the concrete walls, the distant rumble of traffic. I pause, taking in the surroundings, before stepping out into the fading daylight, the city's evening rhythm already beginning.

As I make my way to the parking lot, someone bumps into me. It's a woman. She's visibly upset and devastated. She bends down to retrieve her fallen belongings, and I instinctively kneel to help her. She mumbles an apology, her voice cracking, her eyes teary, as I hand her things back. "Is everything okay?" I ask, my voice calm.

She stares at me for about seven seconds, her eyes wide and red-rimmed, before finally saying, "Yeah, everything's fine," as a tear traces a path down her left cheek. She quickly wipes it away and starts to walk past me. I watch her go, her figure fading into the dim corners of the parking lot. She seems fragile, vulnerable. I stand there for a moment, letting the scene sink in before making my move. People pass by, oblivious to the brief drama that has just unfolded. My usual facade remains intact: cool, collected, and utterly unassuming.

I follow her at a distance, keeping to the shadows, my senses honed to every movement around me. Her distress is palpable, a heavy cloud around her, and I don't want to exacerbate it by startling her. She reaches her car, fumbling with her keys. I approach, close enough to offer a presence, but not so close as to alarm her.

"Hey," I call out, my voice calm and reassuring, cutting through the hum of the parking lot. "Are you sure you're okay? I can call someone if you need help."

She turns, startled. A flicker of unease crosses her eyes, but she attempts a smile, a weak, forced curve of her lips. "I appreciate it, but I'll manage." It's clearly a forced smile. Something is definitely off. Her troubles pique my curiosity, pulling me deeper into the unfolding situation. I simply nod, a feigned understanding on my face. "Alright, just making sure." I pause, gauging her reaction, the subtle shifts in her expression. "Take care."

I start to walk away when she calls out, "Excuse me!"

I turn to see her walking towards me, a newfound determination in her stride. She stops a couple of steps away, her gaze searching mine. "If you don't mind, can we talk over a cup of coffee?"

I hadn't seen that coming, but it's an opportunity. "Yeah, sure," I say, a small, encouraging smile on my face, and lead her to a nearby coffee shop, its warm glow inviting in the fading light.

"Am Jessica, by the way." She says.

"Well, it's nice to meet you, Jessica," is all I offer.

She buys us coffee while I find a seat near the window, the soft light illuminating the quiet corner. As she approaches the table with two steaming cups, I say, "I could've paid for the coffee, you know."

She smiles, a genuine smile this time, a fragile beauty. "That's alright. You drove us here. We're even."

"But I drove us here in your car. I don't see how we're even."

"Fair enough. Just think of it as a thank you. For what's about to happen," she says, her eyes holding a glint of something unreadable.

"Uh... what is about to happen?" I ask, my brows furrowing slightly.

"Letting my emotions out to a stranger. Venting, if you will," she clarifies, her gaze dropping to her coffee cup. I don't speak, unsure how to respond, so I simply nod, inviting her to continue. Breaking the awkward silence, she speaks again, her voice a little stronger. "You must be wondering why I chose you. I mean, you cared enough to check up on me twice. So, I thought, here's a chance for me to let it all out to someone who doesn't know me. So, here we are." She lets out a small, almost imperceptible laugh, more of a sigh, a release of tension.

"For the next sixty minutes, I'm all ears. Vent all you want. I'm ready," I say, folding my arms as a gesture of readiness for whatever I'm about to hear, my expression unwavering.

"Okay," she says with a noticeable sigh, taking a long breath and exhaling slowly, as if preparing herself. "Do you ever feel like life has its plans, ones that we can't control?"

I blink twice, considering her question. "Yes, sometimes, I guess," I reply, my voice quiet. Her eyes glisten with unshed tears, revealing a vulnerability she rarely shows, a raw edge to her composure.

"I've been married for years," she continues, her voice barely above a whisper, her gaze fixed on the steam rising from her coffee. "But... I can't conceive. We've tried everything, and nothing seems to work."

A heavy silence hangs between us, the weight of her confession palpable, filling the space. She speaks with raw honesty, baring a part of her soul to a stranger she'll never see again, a fleeting moment of intimacy.

"I put on a brave face, you know," she murmurs, her fingers trembling around the coffee cup. "I smile, I go about my day, but inside... it's a constant ache that no one sees. Not even my husband. Maybe because I try so hard not to let it show." I listen intently, sensing the depth of her pain, the silent struggles she carries alone. But my mind is already wandering with other thoughts, connecting threads.

"Sometimes, it feels easier to confide in a stranger," she confesses softly, her gaze fixed on a distant point outside the window, as if speaking to the world beyond. "There's a freedom in anonymity. No judgments, no expectations."

I nod in understanding, offering a gentle, empathetic smile. "I'm sorry for what you're going through," I say, trying to sound sincere, offering solace in a moment of shared vulnerability.

She manages a faint smile in return, a fleeting moment of gratitude visible on her face. With a silent nod, she composes herself, pulling the mask she wears so well back into place, concealing her inner turmoil once more. "I..." she hesitates, her voice almost a whisper, but continues anyway. "I even... I even tried to end it once. I feel like there's nothing to live for. I mean, I do love my husband. And he loves me more than I could ask for. But sometimes, it just hurts me I can't give him a family and that hurts. I give up every time I realize that I can't have children of my own."

There it is. Finally. The words I've been waiting for.

She shakes her head, as if sensing she has shared too much, a sudden self-consciousness. "I'm grateful for the temporary release in the presence of a sympathetic stranger," she says with a saddening smile, a bittersweet acknowledgment. "Thank you for listening to me. Let's go." She rises to leave, pushing her chair back with a soft scrape.

"You know, if it's that hard, to the point where you tried to end yourself, you should just go on with that plan again. Maybe that's the only solution after all. Give up." I sound just as sincere as I had moments ago, my voice calm and even.

She stares at me, utter confusion and, what I perceive as, terror etched on her face. Her eyes are wide, unblinking. "Excuse me? You're kidding, right?" she whispers, her voice barely audible.

I rise, move closer to her, and say, "Absolutely not," with an assuring smile, my gaze steady.

VI
Daniel

I drag myself home, exhaustion and frustration a heavy cloak around me. The front door clicks shut with a soft thud, a stark contrast to the cacophony of my mind. I peel off my coat, its weight mirroring the weariness that drapes over me like a heavy cloak. Each step towards the living room is a struggle, my muscles protesting, my nerves frayed. The day has been a relentless assault of frustrations and unanswered questions, leaving me utterly drained. I practically collapse onto the plush cushions of the couch, the soft material offering a fleeting moment of solace.

"Jessica?" I call out, my voice raspy from disuse, a faint hope clinging to the sound. Silence. The house echoes with it, a stark reminder of her absence. She isn't home yet. A heavy sigh escapes my lips, deflating me further. I pinch the bridge of my nose, a familiar ritual in moments of intense stress, hoping to alleviate the throbbing behind my eyes. The thought of waiting for her, of simply sitting there, feels like an insurmountable task, but the weariness in my bones wins out. My eyelids, heavy as lead, flutter shut, and the world dissolves into a hazy, dreamless void.

When I awake, startled, I check the time: fifteen minutes past midnight. Panic, cold and sharp, begins to prickle at the edges of my exhaustion. I rush to our bedroom. "Jess? Honey, you home?" No response. I check the kitchen, then the bathroom. Nothing. She isn't here.

Back in the living room, I fumble for my phone and try calling her. No answer. I try again and again, but the screen remains blank, no connection. I fall back onto the couch, my reflection staring back at me from the dark screen, etched with concern. I shake off the unsettling feeling and send a text. Minutes stretch into an hour, then two, but still no reply. I keep checking my phone, but it remains stubbornly blank.

"Where could she be? It's not like her to stay out this late without letting me know. Maybe her phone died, or she lost track of time. She'll be back soon," I reassure myself, though a strange unease gnaws at me, a cold knot in my stomach.

Hours crawl by, marked only by the ticking of the grandfather clock in the hall, but still no call, no sign of her. "Where are you, Jess?" I murmur, anxiety coiling in my gut. I sigh deeply, pacing the room, the floorboards creaking under my restless feet. All the recent cases at work, the baffling disappearances, only amplify my fear, turning every shadow into a potential threat. Grabbing my car keys, I head out into the pre-dawn chill, determined to search for her.

I search everywhere imaginable: the places she frequented, the homes of friends she might have met. Nothing. Absolutely nothing. "Damnit!" I shout, kicking the bumper of my car, the metallic clang echoing in the silent street.

"Hey!" Jack calls out, jogging towards me, his breath fogging in the cold air. "Any news on Jess yet?" I shake my head, the movement heavy with despair.

"Where on earth could she be?" he mumbles, more to himself than to me, his voice laced with worry.

"She's never done this before. No matter where she went, or how late it was, she'd always let me know. This is so unlike her, and that's what scares me," I say, my pacing quickening, a frantic energy coursing through me.

"Hey, we're going to find her. Don't worry," Jack tries to console me, his hand resting on my shoulder.

I take a deep breath, attempting to calm my racing heart. Jack's words offer some comfort, a fleeting warmth, but the worry still gnaws at the edges of my mind. "I know, I know," I reply, forcing a small smile. "Thanks, Jack. I appreciate your help."

Together, we continue our search, combing through every corner of the neighborhood, desperately hoping for any trace of Jessica. As minutes bleed into hours, the weight of uncertainty grows heavier with each passing moment, crushing my spirit.

Suddenly, my phone rings, shattering the tense silence, making me jump. I scramble to answer, my hand trembling, praying it's Jessica, calling to tell me she's safe. But it isn't her.

"Hello?" I answer, my voice strained with anticipation, my heart pounding.

"Hey, it's Officer Ramirez from the local precinct," the voice on the other end says, calm and professional, but the words hit me like a physical blow. "We found a car registered to Jessica parked on the side of the road a few miles from here. It's been here for a while now. There doesn't seem to be anyone inside." My heart sinks at the news, a chilling dread filling me, and I exchange a worried glance with Jack. "There were two phone numbers. I tried the first one, but there was no response, so I called your number."

"Yes, yes, I—I'm her husband. I'll be right there, officer." I hang up, the phone feeling impossibly heavy in my hand, and without hesitation, we rush to the location Officer Ramirez has given us, our minds racing with fear and uncertainty. As we arrive, my worst fears materialize. Jessica's car sits abandoned by the side of the road, cold and empty. Across the street, a familiar coffee shop stands silently, its windows dark. Maybe she was here. And then?

Panic grips me, a terrifying realization that she could be in serious trouble, that something truly awful has happened. "Where is she?" I whisper, my voice trembling, barely audible. Jack places a reassuring hand on my shoulder, his grip firm. "We'll find her," he says, his voice low and steady, his eyes reflecting a steely determination, a shared resolve.

Together, we join the officers, combing through the area, searching for any clue that might lead us to Jessica's whereabouts. With each passing moment, the sense of urgency intensifies, pushing us to search even harder, against the fading light of dawn. But as the night wears on and the sun finally begins to paint the sky, Jessica remains missing, her fate unknown. The fear and uncertainty weigh heavily on my heart as I pray for her safe return, hoping against hope that she is out there somewhere, waiting to be found, and that none of my worst imaginings have come true.

VII

Joseph

The abandoned laboratory in the basement is shrouded in darkness, the only illumination coming from a flickering overhead light. It casts eerie shadows across the room, creating an atmosphere of dread and anticipation. I stand at the entrance, my pulse racing with excitement as I gaze upon my latest subject. Jessica.

She lies motionless on the cold metal table, her wrists and ankles bound tightly with ropes. I approach her slowly, in my white lab coat, wearing gloves, and a mask. I bring along my tools as I near her.

The anticipation of what is to come, sends a shiver down my spine, and I can barely contain my excitement. Jessica begins to stir, her eyelids fluttering as consciousness returns to her. Panic flashes in her eyes as she takes in her surroundings, her struggles futile against the restraints that bind her to the table. I watch with a sense of satisfaction as she tries to scream, only to be silenced by the tape that covers her mouth. As I draw closer, I can see the fear and confusion in Jessica's eyes, and it fuels the fire within me. I reach for the knife at my side, relishing the weight of it in my hand as I approach her. "Now that you're here, let's can begin." I make small, precise cuts along her arms and legs, savoring the sight of blood that pools beneath her skin. Each cry of pain only serves to fuel my excitement, and I revel in the sense of power that courses through me.

"You see, Jessica," I continue, my voice low and menacing. "I tried to help you. I offered you a way out of your suffering. But you chose to ignore me, to reject my offer of salvation. And now, you must face the consequences." I watch as Jessica's eyes widen in terror, her struggles growing more frantic as she realizes the true extent of her predicament. But it is too late for her now – she is trapped, helpless to resist the fate that awaits her. With a cruel smile, I raise the knife high above my head, relishing the moment before the final blow. Jessica's eyes meet mine, filled with a mixture of fear and resignation, and I know that she understands what is about to happen. "This is for your own good, Jessica," I whisper, my voice barely audible over the pounding of my own heart. "This is the only way to end your suffering."

And with that, I bring the knife down, plunging it deep into Jessica's chest. A strangled cry escapes her lips as pain rips through her body, but it is soon silenced as darkness claims her. I watch with satisfaction as the life drains from her eyes, leaving behind nothing but a hollow shell. "Well, this is what you get for trying to end it all," I sneer, my voice dripping with contempt. "Now, have fun in the afterlife."

As I stand over Jessica's lifeless body, a sense of triumph washes over me. Just like it does each time I succeed. But even as I revel in my success, I know that there are others out there, others who will benefit from my work – and I will stop at nothing to find them.

VIII
Daniel

The sun, a cruel mockery of hope, begins its slow ascent, painting the city streets in hues of gold and rose. But for me, there is no light, no warmth – only an impenetrable darkness, a suffocating despair that clings to my soul. Each tick of the clock is a hammer blow, driving my anxiety deeper, gnawing at the edges of my sanity like a relentless, unseen predator.

I pace the length of the living room, a caged animal, my footsteps wearing paths on the polished floorboards. My mind, a frantic kaleidoscope of fears, is consumed by thoughts of Jessica. Where can she be? What unspeakable horror might have befallen her? The unanswered questions are a physical weight, pressing down on my chest, threatening to suffocate me with their relentless torment. Every shadow seems to hold a sinister secret, every creak of the house a phantom whisper of her name.

Jack sits beside me, a silent sentinel, his presence a small, fragile comfort in the swirling vortex of my turmoil. He offers quiet words, gentle assurances, but even his unwavering support cannot ease the raw, gnawing ache that grips my soul. Jessica is out there somewhere, alone and vulnerable, and I, a detective who prides himself on finding answers, am utterly powerless to help her. The helplessness is a bitter poison, seeping into every fiber of my being.

As the day wears on, a sense of dread, unlike anything I have ever experienced, settles deep within me. It is a cold, creeping certainty that something truly terrible has happened. Each passing hour brings with it a fresh wave of fear and uncertainty, driving me closer and closer to the brink of madness. My hands tremble, my breath hitches, and the world outside the window seems to mock my internal chaos with its indifferent normalcy.

I try to distract myself, to force my mind to focus on anything other than the haunting, indelible image of Jessica's empty car, abandoned by the side of the road. I pick up a book, only to find the words blurring into an incomprehensible mess. I walk to the kitchen, then back to the living room, my movements aimless, driven only by the desperate need to escape the suffocating grip of her absence. But no matter how hard I try, her absence looms over me like a dark, oppressive cloud, casting a shadow over every thought, every action.

Hours bleed into days, each one a testament to the agonizing passage of time, and still, there is no sign of Jessica. My fellow detectives, their faces etched with a shared weariness, continue their relentless search, combing through every inch of the city, every alley, every forgotten corner, in a desperate bid to find her. But as the days stretch into weeks, the initial surge of hope begins to wither, replaced by a chilling sense of resignation and a despair so profound it threatens to consume me whole. This is it, I realize with a sickening lurch in my stomach. This is exactly like all those cold cases, the ones that haunt my dreams, the faces of the missing forever etched into my memory, the answers forever out of reach. The bitter taste of failure, so familiar from my professional life, now mingles with a personal grief that is unbearable.

I cling to the faintest glimmer of hope, a microscopic spark in the vast darkness, praying for Jessica's safe return with every fiber of my being. But deep down, in the quiet, desolate corners of my heart, I know the truth – that she is gone, lost to me forever in a cruel, incomprehensible twist of fate. I sink deeper into the abyss of despair, consumed by grief and regret. I replay our last moments together over and over in my mind, a tormenting loop, searching for some hidden clue, some overlooked sign that could explain her disappearance, that could bring her back.

But there is nothing, only silence, a vast, echoing emptiness where once there had been love and laughter. I find myself haunted by memories of Jessica, her infectious laughter echoing in the empty rooms of our home, a cruel, beautiful reminder of everything I have lost, everything that has been stolen from me.

Yet, even in the depths of this crushing sorrow, a flicker of defiance ignites within me. I can't just sit here and sob. Not yet. Not while there is even the slightest, most improbable chance that she is alive, out there somewhere. If that chance exists, I will investigate with every ounce of my being, workday and night, sacrificing sleep, sanity, everything.

I will find you, Jess.

IX

Joseph

The heavy front door swings inward, revealing the familiar sanctuary of my home. As I step over the threshold, a wave of profound relief washes over me, a stark contrast to the turbulent storm raging within. And there, a beacon of unwavering loyalty, is Mr. Whiskers. He sits poised on the worn welcome mat, his emerald eyes fixed on me, tail twitching with a gentle, rhythmic anticipation that instantly brings a sense of calm to my racing thoughts. He's a small, furry anchor in a world that feels increasingly unmoored.

I kneel, extending a hand, and he immediately rubs against my leg, a soft purr rumbling deep in his chest. Scooping him up, I bury my face in the soft, silken fur of his neck, inhaling the comforting scent of home and catnip. His contented vibrations resonate through me, a gentle balm to the turmoil that has consumed me for days. I carry him deeper into the house, the familiar scent of old books and brewing tea greeting me, a comforting embrace after the cold, sterile world outside. The muted light filtering through the living room windows casts long, gentle shadows, softening the sharp edges of my anxieties.

I set Mr. Whiskers down gently on the cool tile of the kitchen floor, and he stretches languidly before padding off with a quiet dignity towards his favourite sunbeam by the window. There, he curls into a perfect, ginger crescent, eyes half-closed, already drifting into a peaceful nap. Watching him, a small, genuine smile touches my lips for the first time in what feels like an eternity. I walk into my bedroom, the space a haven of soft blues and muted grays and allow myself to simply be. I shed the invisible cloak of darkness that has clung to me, the grim thoughts of my work, the unsettling encounters, the constant hum of the world's suffering. Here, in this quiet space, I consciously embrace the light, the simple, uncomplicated peace that surrounds me.

As I settle into the worn armchair by the window, the warmth of the late morning sun streams through the glass, bathing me in a gentle, golden glow. I close my eyes, listening to the soft, rhythmic purring of Mr. Whiskers from his sun-drenched perch, a tiny, contented engine of peace. The comforting aroma of a freshly brewed pot of Earl Grey tea wafts from the kitchen, a promise of warmth and quiet contemplation. I savour the moment, the delicate scent of bergamot, the gentle warmth of the mug in my hands, the soft weight of the silence.

For today, I take the day off from school and am content to set aside the dark thoughts, the complex equations, the chilling experiments. Today, I revel in the simple, profound tranquillity of the present moment. Today, I am Joseph, not the twisted elementary teacher who lurks in the shadows, burdened by the weight of the ethics of his ambition. Today, I am simply a man who seeks peace, a brief respite in the midst of chaos. And so, I spend the rest of the day in quiet contemplation, savouring the easy company of my beloved cat, allowing myself to bask in the serene embrace of my newfound sanctuary.

Later, a gentle hunger stirs, pulling me towards the kitchen. The rhythmic thwack-thwack-thwack of the knife against the cutting board is surprisingly soothing as I chop vibrant green peppers and sweet red onions with practiced ease, preparing a simple breakfast of fluffy scrambled eggs and golden-brown toast. The sizzle of butter in the pan, the aroma of eggs cooking, the faint scent of toast browning – each sensory detail grounds me, pulling me further into the present, away from the swirling anxieties of the past and future.

After breakfast, a rare indulgence calls to me. I draw a warm bath, the water gushing into the tub with a comforting roar, filling the air with fragrant bubbles of lavender and chamomile. As I sink into the steaming water, the warmth envelops me, a gentle embrace. I close my eyes, letting out a contented sigh, feeling the stresses of the outside world, the lingering tension in my shoulders, the tightness in my jaw, slowly melt away, dissolving into the soothing embrace of the bath.

Emerging refreshed, my skin tingling, I spend the afternoon entirely devoted to Mr. Whiskers. We play with his favourite feather toy, his agile leaps and playful pounces bringing a genuine, unadulterated joy to my heart. His playful antics, his soft nudges for attention, fill the quiet corners of the house with a warmth I haven't realized I'm missing. As the sun begins its slow descent, painting the room in hues of soft orange and deep purple, I settle onto the couch, Mr. Whiskers curled contentedly in my lap, his purr a gentle, rhythmic lullaby. With a contented sigh, I bid farewell to another day of unexpected tranquillity, a day where peace has found its way back to me. I look forward to whatever tomorrow might bring, not with dread, but with a quiet, renewed sense of calm.

X

Daniel

I stare at the empty space beside me on the couch, the phantom weight of Jessica's presence a cruel ache in my chest. As a detective, I've witnessed my fair share of missing person cases, each one a stark lesson in the agonizing futility of an unsolved disappearance. They always end the same way: in echoing silence, in empty rooms, and in unanswered questions that haunt the living for years to come, carving indelible scars on the souls of those left behind. But Jessica's disappearance is a gaping wound, far more personal, more devastating. She's my wife, my soulmate, the very bedrock of my existence. And yet, despite every desperate effort, every resource I can muster, I can't unearth a single clue that might lead me to her.

I've scoured the sprawling city from its gleaming skyscrapers to its forgotten alleyways, chasing down every fragile lead, dissecting every whispered rumor. My phone has become an extension of my hand, each call a gamble, each unanswered ring a fresh stab of disappointment. But every street I turn down, every door I knock on, leads only to another crushing dead end, piling frustration upon heartache. It's as if she's vanished into thin air, leaving behind nothing but the ghost of memories and a litany of unanswered prayers. The empathy I'd once felt for the families of victims is no longer an abstract concept; it's a raw, searing pain. Now, I understand intimately the silent torment they endure. Days have blurred into a suffocating eternity, and I have nothing.

As the days turn into weeks, a chilling sense of helplessness, unlike anything I've ever experienced, consumes me. It's a gnawing, insidious feeling that seeps into my bones, paralyzing me. Every lead I chase, every witness I interview, only serves to deepen the impenetrable mystery surrounding Jessica's disappearance. It's as if the universe itself is conspiring against me, taunting me with its profound and agonizing silence.

I try to push aside the rising tide of fear, to force my mind to focus solely on the relentless task at hand: finding my wife. But the nagging voice in the back of my mind refuses to be silenced, whispering insidious doubts and grim possibilities that threaten to overwhelm me. *She's gone. You failed.* The insidious thoughts claw at my resolve, but I cling fiercely to the belief that I cannot, would not, give up. I have to find her. I have to know what happened.

"Here's your coffee, Dan," Jack's voice cuts through the haze of my thoughts, pulling me back to the precinct's drab reality. He sets the steaming mug on my desk.

"Thanks, man—" I pause, the word "coffee" reverberating in my mind. Coffee. Coffee shop. A jolt goes through me. Her car. Jessica's abandoned car. It had been parked right by a coffee shop. How could I have overlooked such a direct connection? Maybe someone there has seen her, has a fragment of information, anything. "I got it. Let's go." Jack, sensing the urgency in my voice, follows without a single question.

We drive in strained silence; the city lights a blur. I pull the cruiser to a halt outside the Bean Haven coffee shop, its cheerful, looping neon sign flickering mockingly in the window. It's a quaint, small place, cozy and unassuming. The bell above the door jingles as Jack and I step inside, the warm, earthy aroma of roasted coffee beans enveloping us, a stark contrast to the cold dread tightening my gut. The place is nearly empty, save for a few lone figures hunched over laptops, their faces illuminated by the glow of their screens.

I approach the counter, where a young woman with short, vibrantly dyed-pink hair is diligently wiping down the gleaming surface. "Hi there," I begin, my voice betraying a raw desperation I hadn't intended. "I'm looking for some information. My wife, Jessica, went missing days ago." I pull out my phone, showing her a picture of Jessica's smiling face. "I think she was here the day she disappeared. Do you remember seeing her?"

The barista studies the photo, her brow furrowed in thought. "No, I don't think I've seen her here. But let me check with the others, just in case." She disappears into the back, returning moments later with two other staff members. I show them the picture, and one of them, a lanky guy with tattoos snaking up his arms, shakes his head. "We work rotational shifts here, and none of us recall seeing her. Though there is one guy who isn't in today. But I'm sure he wouldn't know anything either."

"Who is it? Can you tell me when he might be back?" I press, a sliver of hope, however faint, igniting within me.

"Well, his name is Justin, and he hasn't been here for a few days. He said he was going out of town for personal reasons," the tattooed barista responds.

"Can I have his contact information?" I ask, my voice edged with authority. They exchange glances, hesitating. "It's okay, I'm a detective. You can share it with me."

"No, that's not it," one of them says, shrugging. "He doesn't have a phone."

"What? He doesn't have a phone? How is that even possible? Who doesn't have a phone these days?" I say, a dubious note creeping into my tone.

"I know, right? That guy is super weird," the pink-haired barista chimes in, confirming my immediate suspicion.

"Well, is there any other way I could get in touch with him? His address, perhaps?" I ask, refusing to let this lead go.

"Uh, no one really knows where he lives. But we do know he's really into video games, and he goes to the video game center down the street every weekend," the tattooed guy offers, a helpful glint in his eye. "Today's Friday. He'll probably show up there tomorrow."

"Alright, thanks for your time, guys," I say, already turning to leave. Jack is waiting by the car. I toss him the keys. "Go to the video game center down the street and ask around for details about a kid named Justin." I start walking in the opposite direction, prompting him to ask, "Where are you headed?"

"I'm going to ask around for some more information myself. Call me when you find something about that kid," I say, picking up my pace. My eyes scan the street.

A few blocks down, I notice the bright, primary colors of Elmwood Elementary School, its playground equipment glinting in the late afternoon sun. A bell rings, signaling dismissal, and a stream of children, their laughter echoing through the air, begins to spill out onto the sidewalk, heading home. I'm so focused on scanning their faces, looking for any lingering adult who might have seen something, that I'm not watching where I'm going.

Suddenly, I bump hard into someone. "Whoa, sorry about that!" I say, instinctively steadying them with a hand on their arm.

"No worries, my fault," a calm, even voice replies. I glance up and see a man with neatly combed dark hair and a precise, almost clinical, demeanour. He gives a brief, polite nod, his eyes distant, as if his mind is already miles away. I offer a quick "Alright then," and he continues on his way, walking against the tide of children who wave and say, "Bye, Mr. Garry!" He must be a teacher. My mind immediately returns to my desperate search, the brief encounter already fading into the background of my overwhelming worry.

A taco van catches my attention. A middle-aged man with a warm smile is handing out steaming tacos to a small line of customers. When he sees me approach, he offers, "Care for a taco, mister?"

"Uh, no thanks. I'm actually here for some information. It's regarding my wife. My missing wife, Jessica," I say, showing him the picture on my phone. "Have you seen her around here?"

He squints at the photo, then at my face. "She does look familiar," he muses. Hope, sharp and electrifying, courses through my body like adrenaline.

"Where did you see her? When exactly?" I press; my voice tight with desperate urgency. He takes his time, his gaze distant, as if sifting through memories.

"Oh, I don't know. She might have bought some taco from me for all I know. I see a lot of people everyday, so pardon me not remembering the exact details," he says in a boring tone.

"Thanks for your help," I say, and pull out my phone to call Jack. "Stay at the video game center. I am on my way."

As I reach the corner, a figure detached itself from the crowd. It's Jack. "That kid, Justin? He's here. I haven't gone up to him yet."

"I thought he came here during the weekends. Well, good for us. Let's go," I say, my pulse quickening. We approach Justin, who is deeply immersed in his game, headphones clamped over his ears. He's so absorbed, so completely detached from the world around him, that he has no idea we've been standing behind him for almost two full minutes. My patience, thin from days of anxiety, snaps. I reach out and pull the headphones from his head.

"Hey, kid. We just need a couple of minutes of your time. Then we'll be out of your hair, and you can return to your video games, alright?" I say, trying to sound calm, but the urgency in my voice is undeniable. He looks from me to Jack, then back to me, his eyes wide with surprise and a flicker of fear. He seems nervous, perhaps afraid, unable to speak.

Jack, ever the calming presence, immediately steps in. "There's nothing to fear, kid. We just want to ask you a few questions. Would you answer them for us?" He gives a tiny, almost imperceptible nod, which barely counts, but we take it as a yes.

I show him Jessica's picture on my phone. "Have you ever seen her before?" I ask. He barely glances at the photo, his head turning quickly to the side. I can sense the tension radiating from him, his eyeballs dart rapidly from side to side, like a trapped animal. He definitely knows something. Jack pulls up a chair and sits across from him, leaning in.

"Listen, kid. If you know something, please tell us. This woman is his wife, and she's been missing for weeks now.

Any information would be helpful, so don't hold back. You've got nothing to fear. Trust us."

"I-I know nothing. Sorry, I can't help you." The words tumble out in a rush, and then, before I can react, the kid pushes past me and bolts for the door. Jack starts to run after him, but I stop him. "Let me go after him."

I step out, seeing Justin pacing quickly, not running, but walking with a strange, agitated speed. Perhaps he wants to say something but is too afraid. I follow him, matching his pace, not trying to catch him or overtly confront him. He sees me trailing him, yet he doesn't break into a run. It's clear: he wants to tell me something. Or maybe, show me something? Where is this kid going anyway? For what felt like an eternity, he keeps walking, and I keep following, a silent, tense pursuit.

After a few more steps, he halts abruptly. I wait, holding my breath, for him to move. He doesn't budge. I slowly near him, closing the distance. He remains still, his back to me. He's finally ready to talk. I'm almost directly behind him when he suddenly whirls around. "She looked frightened."

My heart plummets, hitting rock bottom.

Who the hell was she with?

Why was she here?

Is she okay?

All these thoughts scream in my head, a frantic prayer, as I wait for Justin to say more. He stands motionless for a long moment, then meets my gaze directly, his eyes wide, as though he's weighing his next words with immense care. The street is hushed, save for the distant hum of traffic and the occasional mournful honk of a horn. I feel my pulse thudding a frantic rhythm in my ears, urging him to speak, to deliver the truth, no matter how painful. He takes a shaky breath.

"She... she didn't seem like she wanted to be there," he whispers, his voice barely audible, a fragile thread in the quiet street. My heart skips a beat, a cold fear clawing its way up my throat.

"What do you mean? Was she in danger? Did someone take her?" I demand, trying to keep my voice steady, though the panic is rising, threatening to overwhelm me.

Justin bites his lip, shifting his weight from foot to foot, clearly uncomfortable, tormented by what he knows. "I don't know. I only saw her for a few seconds. She was with this guy. He looked... I don't know... important? Maybe rich?"

"Did you hear anything they said? Did they talk to each other?" I press, my voice now laced with desperate urgency, sensing we're on the precipice of something critical.

Justin shakes his head. "Not really. He had his hand on her arm, kind of tight. They walked into the alley next to the coffee shop. I didn't follow them. I didn't think it was my business. But she—" He stops, looking down at his feet, the guilt in his eyes palpable, a heavy burden.

"What? Justin, what is it?" I step closer, barely able to contain my desperation, my voice a low growl.

Justin hesitates, his fingers twitching nervously at his sides. His eyes dart around, as if afraid someone might be listening, watching. He leaned in just slightly, lowering his voice to a conspiratorial whisper.

"She looked at me," he says, his voice barely a breath. "Just for a second. But... her eyes—" He swallows hard, a visible struggle. "She was scared. Like she wanted to scream but couldn't."

A chill, icy and sharp, snaked down my spine. My pulse hammered in my ears, a frantic drumbeat against my eardrums. "Then what happened?" I ask, my voice barely a whisper, afraid of the answer.

Justin shifts uneasily; his gaze fixed on the asphalt. "They disappeared into the alley... and she never came back out. I feel like it could've been stopped if I had stepped up, but I was scared. I am sorry!" he pleads, his voice cracking, tears welling in his eyes.

The world tilts on its axis. My breath catches in my throat, a searing pain. I turn slowly; my gaze drawn to the dark, narrow alley leading down to a forgotten path. My wife. My Jessica.

I turn back to Justin, reaching out to pat his shoulder, offering what comfort I can, even as my own world crumbles. "It's not your fault, kid. You were right not to step up. He could have hurt you as well. But you could have informed the cops about this. I get that you were scared. But it's always best to let the adults know of such things. Thanks for telling the truth now. You may go."

He nods apologetically, his head bowed, then turns and paces away, faster and faster, leaving me standing there with what some people would call a chilling sense of dread. But for me, it's far more. It's a cold, hard certainty.

I finally have a lead. And I know where to go next.

XI

Joseph

I hear her laughter before I see her. It's a sound spun from sunlight and pure joy, light and melodic, bouncing through the unnatural stillness of the park. It weaves itself into the crisp evening air, a forgotten melody suddenly plucked from the depths of memory. There's something achingly familiar about the sound, something that tugs at a deep, unnamed part of me, a place long since walled off.

I look up, my gaze sweeping across the verdant expanse, and there she is.

Her small feet, clad in bright red sneakers, barely make a sound against the winding asphalt path as she runs ahead of me, weaving effortlessly between the towering, ancient trees. Her golden hair, caught by the gentle breeze, streams out behind her like a spun halo.

"Hey," I call out, my voice, despite my effort, sounding thin and reedy in the empty space. "Not too far."

She doesn't respond. Doesn't even turn her head, her focus absolute on her carefree flight. She just keeps running, her small arms spread wide like she's pretending to be an airplane, utterly unburdened, utterly joyful.

A strange, prickling unease begins to creep into my chest. The park is empty—too empty. There's no distant chatter of other families, no cheerful barks of dogs, no chirping of birds hidden in the branches, no gentle rustling of leaves in the canopy above. Just silence. A profound, unnatural silence that doesn't belong in a place meant for laughter and play. It's the kind of silence that precedes a storm, or worse.

I quicken my pace, my strides lengthening, a frantic energy building beneath my skin. The wind, which had moments ago been a gentle caress, picks up, turning cold and biting against my exposed skin, raising goosebumps.

"Hey, sweetheart," I try again, my voice laced with a growing urgency. "Come back here."

Still, she doesn't listen. Doesn't even falter in her effortless run. She's nearing the very edge of the park now, where the well-worn path meets the road—except there is no road. My stomach twists violently, a knot of icy dread coiling in my gut.

Where there should be solid asphalt and neatly painted sidewalks, there is nothing. A void. A yawning abyss, stretching endlessly into an inky blackness that seems to swallow the light, blacker than the darkest, starless night. The sheer, impossible sight of it makes my head spin, a sudden dizzying vertigo seizing me. My pulse quickens, hammering against my ribs like a trapped bird.

She stops. Right at the very edge. Her tiny form silhouetted against the terrifying nothingness.

I freeze, my breath catching in my throat, each beat of my heart a painful thud against my ribs.

She turns to me slowly, her movements unnervingly deliberate. And for the very first time, I see her face clearly.

Wide, fathomless eyes, reflecting the inky blackness behind her. Lips parted, trembling slightly. A silent plea agonizingly trapped somewhere deep in her throat, unable to escape.

She looks... terrified. Utterly, completely terrified. And suddenly, I know. Something is profoundly, terribly wrong.

A violent gust of wind howls through the park, a mournful, agonizing cry, sending a deep, bone-chilling tremor down my spine. She sways slightly, her small frame trembling violently against the sheer force of it, teetering precariously on the brink.

My feet move before my mind can even register the thought. "Wait! Don't move—" The words are ripped from my lungs, desperate, futile.

The ground beneath her, that fragile sliver of earth, simply collapses.

The world tilts violently, a disorienting lurch. My vision blurs, the edges of the park dissolving into a kaleidoscope of green and black. My body moves on pure instinct, a primal surge of adrenaline propelling me forward. I lunge, my arm outstretched, fingers splayed wide, desperately reaching out, my fingertips just grazing the delicate hem of her white dress before—

She's gone.

Swallowed whole by the abyss. Vanished without a trace, without a sound.

A scream, raw and primal, rips from my throat, tearing at my vocal cords. It's a sound born of utter despair, of absolute horror. "NO!"

I drop to my knees at the treacherous edge, shards of unseen rock biting into my skin, unheeded. I peer into the impossible void, my eyes straining against the darkness. There's nothing. No sign of her. No sound, not even a whisper, to indicate she ever existed. Just endless, suffocating blackness. My breath is ragged, my chest heaving, burning with every gasp for air, as I frantically search for something—anything—but I find only emptiness, a crushing, boundless void.

This isn't real. It can't be real. My mind screams the denial, a desperate mantra.

And yet, my hands are shaking uncontrollably, trembling with a cold terror that chills me to the core. My skin is ice cold, clammy with sweat. My heart is hammering against my ribs, a frantic, terrified drumbeat, threatening to tear itself free.

I lost her.

I lost—

My body jerks violently, a sudden, convulsive spasm, and I wake with a sharp gasp, my breath coming in short, ragged bursts. I'm sitting bolt upright in my bed, my hands clutching the damp sheets, soaked through with sweat. My skin is slick, cold. My pulse pounds in my ears, a deafening roar that drowns out everything else, the dream's terrifying echo.

For a long, agonizing moment, I just sit there, rigid, staring into the darkened room, the shadows dancing, trying desperately to remember how to breathe, how to exist. My mind is sluggish, tangled in the lingering, chilling threads of the nightmare.

The girl. Her laughter, so real, so vibrant. The terrifying abyss.

My fingers twitch involuntarily, a phantom sensation. I can still feel the fleeting, desperate brush of fabric against my fingertips, still hear the echo of her laughter—before it abruptly turned to a suffocating silence.

I rake a trembling hand through my sweat-soaked hair, pulling at the roots, and squeeze my eyes shut, willing the images away.

A dream.

No. A nightmare. One that has haunted me for years.

My gaze drifts towards the nightstand, drawn by an invisible force. There, bathed in the soft glow of the digital alarm clock, sits a small, framed photograph.

I reach for it before I can stop myself, my fingers trembling as they close around the cool metal frame.

The girl in the picture is smiling. Her eyes are bright, sparkling with an unbridled joy and life. She's wearing a delicate white dress, twirling in a sun-drenched field.

My little sister.

My *late* sister.

A sharp, ragged exhale leaves my lips, a sound of profound pain, as I tighten my grip on the frame, my knuckles turning white, almost snapping the glass.

She's gone. She's been gone for years.

And no matter how many times I dream of saving her, of reaching her, of pulling her back from the brink, the ending is always the same.

Always.

XII

Daniel

The alley is a gaping maw of shadow, a narrow, suffocating corridor squeezed between two hulking, worn-out brick buildings. The air hangs heavy and stagnant, thick with the faint, metallic scent of damp concrete mingling with the cloying, greasy aroma of stale cooking oil from a nearby dumpster. Discarded wrappers, like forgotten secrets, and a scattering of cigarette butts litter the grimy asphalt, each one a testament to anonymous lives passing through. A single, sickly flickering streetlight at the far end struggles against the encroaching darkness, casting elongated, grotesque shadows that dance and writhe, making the already narrow passage seem to shrink, pressing in on me, claustrophobic and menacing.

Jessica was here? The question is a cold, hard knot in my stomach.

I swallow hard, my throat suddenly dry, my heartbeat drumming a frantic, uneven rhythm against my eardrums. Justin's whispered words replay in my head, a chilling mantra: *She was scared. Like she wanted to scream but couldn't.* The image of her wide, terrified eyes, trapped and silent, flashes before me, a phantom pain.

I reach for my tactical flashlight, the familiar weight of it a small comfort in the burgeoning dread. The click of the switch is unnervingly loud in the oppressive quiet, and a sharp, focused beam of light slices through the gloom, sweeping across the alley. The powerful beam bounces off the slick, graffiti-scarred brick walls, illuminating nothing but layers of grime, streaks of unknown substances, and the unsettling sheen of dampness.

I take a few slow, deliberate steps forward, each one a conscious effort. The crunch of loose gravel and forgotten debris beneath my shoes is unnervingly loud, amplified by the suffocating silence of the night. My pulse quickens with each step, an inexplicable dread settling deep in my gut, a cold, heavy stone.

At first glance, there is nothing out of the ordinary. No overturned trash cans, no scattered belongings, no tell-tale signs of a struggle. The dust on the ground, disturbed only by my own heavy boots, shows no distinct footprints that hint at Jessica's presence. But something feels profoundly, disturbingly off. I can't quite put my finger on it, but the stillness in the air seems unnatural—a breathless, anticipatory quiet, as if this forgotten place is holding its breath, waiting for me to leave, guarding its terrible secret.

I crouch low, my knees protesting, near the precise spot where Justin said he last saw her. My gloved fingers brush against the cold, gritty ground, meticulously searching for anything—anything at all—that could give me a clue. A stray thread of fabric, a fresh scuff mark on the brick, a single, tell-tale hair. But the ground is bare, swept clean by some unseen hand, or perhaps, simply never disturbed.

Frustration, hot and bitter, bubbles in my chest, threatening to erupt. I clench my jaw, the muscles tightening, and turn my attention to the walls. Maybe there are marks? Scratches from fingernails, scuff marks from a shoe, signs that she had been dragged or had resisted? I step closer, pressing my body against the rough brick, running my hand along the cold, unyielding surface. But it is just stone and mortar, as indifferent and unyielding as the silence that surrounds me, offering no answers, no solace.

Straightening, I turn towards the very end of the alley, where a heavy, nondescript metal door stands flush against the brick wall. It's painted a faded, industrial gray, blending almost seamlessly into the grime. No sign, no markings, no indication of what lies beyond. Just a plain handle and a thick, rusted padlock, its shackle gleaming faintly in my flashlight beam. I reach out, my hand closing around the cold metal, and test it—it doesn't budge. It's locked tight, a formidable barrier.

My gut screams at me to push further, to break in if I have to, to tear down this barrier and uncover whatever truth it conceals. But I know better. I'm a detective, not a vigilante. I need proof, not a trespassing charge that could derail the entire investigation. Instead, I knock. Three sharp, insistent raps against the unyielding metal.

Nothing. Only the echo of my own knuckles.

I knock again, harder this time, a desperate, almost frantic rhythm. Still nothing. The silence is deafening.

Pressing my ear against the cold, unyielding surface of the door, I strain to hear anything—a muffled voice, a faint shuffle of movement, the low hum of an appliance, anything to suggest life on the other side. But all I get is a long, loud silence. A cold, empty silence that makes my skin crawl, a premonition of something truly sinister.

I step back, my gaze sweeping across the alley one last time, my flashlight beam dancing over every crack and crevice, every discarded piece of trash. But there is nothing new, nothing revealed.

With a heavy sigh that feels like it's drawn from the very depths of my soul, I turn and go back the way I came, each step a testament to my crushing disappointment. My search tonight has yielded nothing but more questions, more agonizing uncertainty. No tangible trace of her. No clear answers. Just an empty alley, its secrets held tight, offering nothing but despair.

As I step back onto the main street, the city lights, once a comforting beacon, now seem dimmer, colder, their glow muted by the profound darkness that has settled over my world. The city moves on, a relentless, indifferent tide of humanity, as if nothing had happened, as if Jessica had never been here at all, never existed.

But I know better.

And I am not giving up.

Not now. Not ever.

I will find out.

XIII

Joseph

The city, a sprawling, indifferent leviathan, hums its muted, distant symphony of life and death. From somewhere far off, the mournful wail of sirens threads through the urban tapestry, a fleeting, sorrowful note that quickly fades. Overhead, streetlights flicker erratically, sickly orange pools of light battling the encroaching darkness, casting elongated, dancing shadows against the empty, damp sidewalks. I move with a grim, unyielding purpose, my head bowed, my gaze fixed on the cracked pavement before me. My hands, clenched into fists, are shoved deep into the welcoming cold of my coat pockets, seeking a comfort. The biting air gnaws at my exposed skin, a raw, persistent chill that promises deeper cold, but I barely register its sting; my focus is singular, absolute, consuming every other sensation.

~~~

The alley. It is darker, narrower, more oppressive than I remember, a suffocating chasm between two colossal brick behemoths. The walls are slick with an unseen dampness, choked by layers of faded graffiti, vibrant colours bleeding
~~~

into faded shadows, and the tattered remnants of old posters, peeling at the edges like decaying flesh. A single, diseased fluorescent light buzzes directly above a monstrous, rusted dumpster, its pallid glow casting grotesque, elongated shadows that writhe across the cracked pavement. The deeper I venture, the more the distant sounds of the city fade, swallowed whole by the encompassing walls, leaving only the oppressive silence that is both familiar and unsettling. I pause at what appears to be a dead end – at least, what appears to be a dead end to anyone else.

My fingers twitch, a nervous tremor, as I scan the ground. The others, the superficial, the untrained, would walk away by now, dismissing this as just another forgotten urban crevice. But this isn't just any alley. This is where I come to exert control, to ensure the world, in its chaotic indifference, never fails me again. This is my sanctuary, my clandestine laboratory, the heart of my grim obsession.

I crouch low, my knees protesting softly, running my hand across the rough, cold concrete. Dirt, the gritty residue of forgotten lives, mixed with ancient cigarette butts, and a few scattered shards of broken glass – nothing overtly unusual. But then, my palm flattens against the ground, just beside a slightly loose tile, seeking the subtle edge. And there it is. A seam. A faint line, barely visible to the untrained eye, practically invisible unless I know precisely what I am searching for, what truth lies beneath.

My pulse quickens, a low, urgent thrumming in my ears, as I dig my gloved fingers into the narrow crevice and pull. With a low, reluctant groan, a sound of ancient metal protesting its disturbance, the hidden trapdoor gives way, revealing a gaping maw of darkness below. A rush of stale air, damp and metallic, billows upwards, carrying with it the undeniable scent of rusted iron and something else—something hauntingly familiar—filling my lungs. The smell of preservation. It has been days, weeks even, since I last descended into this sanctuary. Precisely, since Jessica. Since her disappearance, I haven't been here, not until now. The irony is a bitter taste in my mouth.

I begin my descent, my hand finding the cold, narrow railing. The darkness swallows me whole, absolute and immediate, each step downward a surrender to the unknown. The further down I go, the colder it gets, the chill seeping into my bones, promising what lies ahead. The silence is oppressive, a thick, suffocating blanket that wraps around me like an unseen force. Yet, paradoxically, I am at peace here. This place is mine. It is control.

At the bottom, my foot meets solid concrete. I reach for the switch on the wall, my fingers brushing against the cold plastic. With a low hum and a series of erratic flickers, the dim fluorescent lights above sputter to life, bathing the vast underground space in a pale, sterile glow. The room is exactly as I have left it. A long, gleaming metal workbench, meticulously organized, lined with an array of neatly arranged surgical tools, each one glinting under the harsh light. Towering, cylindrical glass tanks, filled with a clear, faintly bluish liquid, hum softly, their complex displays pulsing with quiet, unwavering efficiency.

Inside the tanks, suspended in their liquid prisons, floating in pristine, almost ethereal condition, are organs. Lungs, intricate and delicate. Hearts, robust and powerful. Kidneys, perfectly formed. All carefully preserved, awaiting their purpose. This is my greatest achievement. My proof that I can do what others can't, what the archaic medical world refuses to fully embrace. While the world wastes precious time searching for fleeting donors, while lives slip away waiting for a miracle, I have found a way to store life itself.

This is my answer. My solution. No one else needs to suffer like I did. Like she did.

I step closer to one of the tanks, resting my gloved hand against the cool, smooth glass. A perfect heart floats within, suspended in the shimmering liquid, its delicate veins visible beneath the surface, a silent testament to biological perfection. A flawless specimen, waiting. I should feel pride, a surge of accomplishment. But instead, a cold, familiar emptiness settles in my chest, a phantom limb where my own heart should have soared.

She should have had this. She would still be here. The thought is a bitter echo of an old, unhealable wound.

A sound, faint but unmistakable, shatters the oppressive silence. A creak.

My body stiffens, every nerve on high alert. I turn my head slightly, listening, my breath held. Nothing. Only the steady hum of the machines. But I know I heard something. My eyes, sharpened by years of vigilance, scan the room. The machines continue their steady hum. The lights flicker overhead, casting their sterile glow. Everything looks precisely as it should. But I am not alone.

I move with a practiced, predatory quiet towards the far side of the room, where tall, industrial metal shelves hold rows of labelled containers—specimens from past projects, meticulous notes, the remnants of past failures and the trophies of successes. There is a shadow there, deeper than the others, cast against the cold concrete wall.

I inhale slowly, silently, pressing my back against the metal workbench, its cool surface against my lab coat. My right hand, almost on instinct, reaches for the scalpel beside me, its polished blade gleaming faintly. Small, impossibly sharp, reliably lethal. My fingers close around the cool metal handle, the familiar weight a comfort.

Another sound. A soft shuffle. Someone breathing. Closer now.

Then—

A crash. The sudden, jarring clamour of metal on concrete.

I move fast, sweeping the scalpel forward in a practiced arc as I lunge toward the source of the sound, toward the deeper shadow. But there is no one there. Just an overturned tray of surgical instruments clattering to the floor, scattered like fallen teeth. My heartbeat thunders in my ears, a frantic drum. I step back, my grip tightening on the scalpel. Someone is here. Someone has knocked that over. But where—

A breath. A sharp intake of air. Right behind me.

I spin around, scalpel raised, just as a figure emerges from the deeper shadows, darting toward the narrow, winding stairs. Instinct, cold and precise, kicks in. I chase after them, my feet pounding against the cold concrete floor, a relentless rhythm. They are fast, surprisingly agile, but I know this place better. This is my domain. The second their hand touches the cold metal railing of the staircase, I lunge, grabbing the back of their jacket with a surge of strength and yanking hard.

They fall backward with a strangled yell, hitting the floor with a sickening thud. I am on them in an instant, pinning them down before they can even begin to recover. My knee presses into their chest, forcing the air from their lungs, and the scalpel, glinting menacingly, is poised at their throat, its razor-sharp tip just millimetres from their jugular.

A pair of wide, terrified eyes stare up at me, reflecting the harsh fluorescent lights. A boy. A teenager, no older than sixteen or seventeen, perhaps. His chest heaves, his breath coming in ragged, desperate gasps, his pupils blown wide with abject fear.

"Who are you?" I demand, my voice low, dangerous, a growl that barely escapes my lips.

He tries to speak, but only a desperate wheeze escapes his throat. I ease the pressure of my knee just enough for him to gasp for air.

"I—I wasn't—" he stammers, his voice thin and reedy. "I was just—I saw you come down here. I was curious—"

"Liar." The word is a flat, cold accusation.

He flinches violently beneath me. My grip on the scalpel tightens almost imperceptibly. "You were watching me. You knew where to look. How?"

He shakes his head quickly, frantically, his whole body trembling beneath my weight. "I swear! I just—I saw you go down the alley. I was gonna leave, but then—then I saw the door."

I study him, my gaze unwavering, searching for any flicker of deceit in his terrified eyes. His pulse is erratic beneath my grip, a frantic flutter, his chest rising and falling in rapid succession. He is scared. Terribly scared. But scared of what? Me? Or something else entirely?

I press the blade just enough for him to feel its chilling kiss on his skin. His breath hitches, a tiny, strangled sound.

"What did you see?" My voice is barely a whisper now, utterly devoid of emotion.

"N-nothing! I swear!" His voice is a desperate squeak.

I exhale slowly, a long, controlled breath, and then press down on his chest harder. His desperate breaths turn to wheezes, then strangled gasps. His body squirms beneath mine, struggling, thrashing weakly, but I don't let up. I can't. Not now. Not when everything is at stake.

"Please—" he chokes, tears welling in his wide eyes. "I won't tell—I swear."

They all say that.

I am sorry, kid.

I twist the scalpel, a swift, practiced motion, slicing deep into the soft flesh of his neck. His body arches violently, a single, strangled gasp escaping his lips, a final, gurgling sound as pain rips through him. Then, with a shudder, he goes still. Warm blood wells up, a shocking crimson against the cold concrete floor, pooling rapidly around his head. His eyes, wide with terror, stare up at the sterile ceiling, unseeing, forever frozen in that final moment of fear.

A shame. A truly wasted opportunity.

I take a deep, steadying breath, calming my pulse, bringing my emotions back under rigid control. It had to be done. He is a loose end, a potential threat to everything I have built, everything I believe in.

With a steady, methodical hand, I drag the surprisingly light body to the far side of the room, near the large industrial freezer.

He'll be useful soon enough.

I glance back at the gleaming tanks, the perfectly preserved organs suspended in their liquid prisons, bathed in the pale, sterile glow.

A new heart.

A new set of lungs and kidneys.

Good organs. Perfect specimens.

Life, waiting to be used. Life, waiting to be given a second chance.

I stare at the cold, lifeless body lying on the floor, its brief, terrified existence now concluded.

And it won't be wasted.

XIV

Daniel

The precinct is a dissonant symphony of controlled chaos. Phones shriek, their urgent rings cutting through the steady murmur of officers' voices. The distant, asthmatic hum of the coffee machine sputters out its last dregs, adding to the low thrum of activity. Yet, I hear none of it. My mind, a tangled knot of anxiety and fragmented memories, refuses to cooperate, stubbornly fixated on the single, agonizing thought of Jess. All my focus, however, is locked onto the couple sitting across from me, their grief a palpable, suffocating presence in the sterile room. The mother clutches a crumpled tissue in her hands, her knuckles white, her face a pale, drawn mask of anguish. The father sits rigid, his jaw clenched, his fingers tapping an anxious, almost frantic rhythm against the armrest of his utilitarian plastic chair.

They don't need to utter a single word. I already know what confession is about to tear from their lips, what fresh wave of despair is about to break.

"Our son—he's missing," the mother finally manages, her voice a fragile, cracking whisper, each syllable a shard of glass. "Justin never stays out this late. He was supposed to be home hours ago. He's never done this before."

Justin?

The name strikes me like a physical blow, a hammer to the chest, stealing the air from my lungs. My fingers, unbidden, tighten around the pen I hold, the plastic groaning under the pressure. My gaze darts to the missing person report they've just filled out, my eyes frantically scanning over the sparse, chilling details: Male, seventeen. Last seen near Sycamore Street.

The alley.

A choked curse dies in my throat.

Shit.

My mind, despite its turmoil, relentlessly pulls up a face—dark, intelligent eyes, a shock of messy hair, a nervous energy that barely masks his underlying determination. I'd seen him just days ago, standing before me, his youth and apprehension a stark contrast to my desperate quest for answers about Jessica. He had been asking about her.

Damn it.

"Detective?" The father's voice, raspy with desperation, snaps me back to the present, his eyes searching mine, silently pleading for reassurance, for a glimmer of hope. I offer none. I couldn't.

"When was the last time you spoke to him?" I ask instead, my voice a practiced monotone, betraying none of the turmoil raging within me.

The mother dabbles at her eyes with the crumpled tissue, a small, choked sob escaping her. "Yesterday morning. He said he had some errands to run. He never told me where. But his friend said they last saw him heading toward downtown."

Downtown. Near the alley.

A cold, heavy weight settles in my gut, dragging me down. I keep my expression meticulously neutral as I scribble notes onto my pad, but my thoughts are racing, colliding like frantic bumper cars. Is this a coincidence? A cruel twist of fate? Or something far more sinister?

"Did Justin mention anything strange recently?" I press, leaning forward slightly, my voice dropping to a low, probing tone. "Anyone bothering him? Anything unusual at all?"

The parents exchange a quick, meaningful glance, a silent communication of shared worry. The father, after a moment of hesitation, speaks, his voice heavy. "Not really. But he did seem... scared. Also, he mentioned feeling guilty about something. Didn't tell us why."

No. No. *No.*

I lean back in my chair, exhaling slowly, a long, shuddering breath. This isn't just another missing person's case. This is connected. Justin had been there. He saw Jessica. Maybe he saw the person who took her, and that person must have captured him too.

I rise to my feet, the slight creak of my chair echoing in the sudden silence of my internal world. "We'll do everything we can to find him. I need you both to stay available in case we have more questions, for anything, no matter how small."

The mother nods weakly; her gaze fixed on some distant point of despair. The father grips my hand in a firm shake, his eyes, bloodshot and filled with a quiet, desperate plea, boring into mine. I watch as they leave the station, their shoulders slumped, their figures shrinking with each step, my mind already spinning through the grim possibilities, connecting the invisible dots.

I grab my coat, the rough fabric a familiar comfort, and head towards the precinct archives, a cavernous space filled with the forgotten echoes of unsolved mysteries. I need to go through the other missing persons' reports again—not just the recent ones, but all of them. I need to see if there is a pattern I have missed, a chilling commonality that had eluded me before. Jessica isn't the first. Justin isn't the last. And I have a chilling feeling I am running out of time.

The files, dusty and cold, spread out before me like a macabre deck of cards, each one representing a life vanished. They paint a grim, horrifying picture: mostly young adults. All disappearing in the same sprawling city. No bodies. No real evidence. Just vanished, leaving behind nothing but aching voids and shattered lives.

And now Justin. A wave of sickening guilt washes over me. This is my fault. I shouldn't have bothered that kid. I shouldn't have pushed him into the path of whatever malevolent force had consumed Jessica.

This isn't just a missing persons case anymore.

This is personal.

This is a hunt.

XV

Joseph

The rain falls soft tonight, a steady, almost comforting murmur against the city's tired skin. It isn't a violent downpour, but a persistent, whispering descent that reminds me, chillingly, of the quiet in a hospital room after someone dies. That breathless stillness, that suffocating hush where everything waits to be acknowledged, every unspoken regret hanging heavy in the air, but no one dares to break the fragile peace with words.

I stand across the street from the Café, the neon sign a hazy blur through the fine mist. A cigarette rests between my fingers, unlit, its paper cylinder a mere prop. I don't smoke often, perhaps once a month, if that. The ritual matters more than the acrid burn of tobacco. It is about control. Precision. I don't let anything consume me unless I choose it, unless I orchestrate its precise entry and exit from my carefully constructed world.

Through the steamed-up glass of the café, I watch him.

The man who has been pacing through my footprints, the determined detective who, like a persistent burrowing insect, has been pulling loose threads from the fabric of my carefully spun truth, trying to weave a narrative that simply doesn't want to be found.

I decided to look him up the moment he bumped into me the other day. He is sharp. The kind of sharp that can cut deep if you underestimate it, if you allow even a flicker of complacency. I've heard the strained, almost raw edge in his voice during press briefings, the way his composure cracks ever so slightly when he speaks about the "missing." He wants justice, perhaps, or maybe just the elusive peace of closure. It is always one or the other with men like him.

Tonight, he is alone. A solitary figure amidst the soft hum of the café. His coffee, steaming gently, remains untouched. His fingers, restless and anxious, thumb through pages of a file. One of my own, I suspect. Likely the latest.

Daniel looks bone-tired, the shadows beneath his eyes stark against his pale skin. But he is alert, every muscle in his body coiled with a restless energy. Grief, a heavy, invisible cloak, seems to coil in his shoulders, pulling them down. Loss doesn't ever truly fade for people like us. It just moves deeper, integrating itself into the very bones, becoming a part of the framework of who you are.

I know that look. I wore it for years after Lily died.

I push open the café door. The bell above it chimes, a weary, hollow sound, like it is tired of being useful, tired of announcing entrances and exits. The immediate rush of warmth is a comforting shock—a fragrant fog of roasted coffee beans, damp coats, and the low murmur of whispered conversations, a familiar symphony of anonymity.

I order a jasmine green tea—a delicate, aromatic blend. I pick a table near his, carefully chosen. Not close enough to alarm him, not close enough to seem predatory, but just enough to observe. Just enough to listen, to gauge his rhythm, his subtle shifts.

He doesn't recognize me. Not truly. Our eyes meet for a fleeting heartbeat, a moment suspended in time, and I feel him pause—that faint flicker of intuition, the subconscious whisper that something is off.

It passes. His gaze drifts back to his file, and I become part of the wallpaper, a blurred figure in his periphery.

Invisible.

Exactly where I want to be.

~~~

Lily's laughter. It echoed in my skull sometimes, so vivid, so startling in its clarity, that it wrenched a gasp from my chest.

She was ten. All freckles and stardust, a riot of ginger curls and a spirit brighter than any constellation. She knew the name of every star in the night sky, believed the moon smiled back at her, a benevolent, silent guardian. She used to draw on the walls of her hospital room, scribble swirling galaxies, fantastical planets, and exploding supernovas in marker, like she was designing a new universe. A universe where she didn't need a new heart.

Her condition was rare, cruel, but manageable—if we found a donor. That was the crushing, unspoken part. The heavy, unsayable truth that hung in the air: *if.* There were endless lists, stacks of sterile paperwork, the hollow platitudes of "we're doing all we can" speeches from sympathetic doctors. But it wasn't enough. It was never enough.

I was in the cold, sterile hallway when her alarms finally screamed their desperate farewell. Nurses ran, their footsteps blurring, their faces grim. My hands, numb and useless, were gripped around the cold steel of the railing.
~~~

And then, silence. A profound, absolute silence that swallowed the frantic beeps and the hurried whispers.

Silence, and the knowing.

Lily died not because death was stronger—but because the system was weaker than the raw, desperate will to save. It was the crushing, indifferent weight of bureaucracy, of scarcity, of a waiting game that ended in the cold embrace of loss.

That's when I stopped believing in waiting lists. That's when the conviction solidified in my soul, cold and unyielding as steel.

That's when I started collecting lives that were already slipping through the cracks, lives that the system had deemed expendable, or simply inconvenient.

Not everyone wanted to live, I had learned. Some people begged to die. They were the broken, the despairing, the ones who saw only darkness. I just... listened. I found them, those lost souls teetering on the precipice, and I eased them out of their suffering. And then, I preserved what they left behind. Their strong, healthy hearts. Their robust kidneys. Their vital lungs. I then delivered them to people who fought, clawing for every precious breath, who wanted to live more than the others wanted to die.

I didn't kill. I facilitated a trade. A necessary, brutal exchange.

~~~

Daniel's phone buzzes, a low vibration against the tabletop. He answers with a clipped tone, his voice low, cautious, a detective's instinct already engaged.

"I don't know. I think we're missing something."

He is close. That excites me more than it should, a dangerous thrill prickling beneath my skin. It isn't fear, not for myself. It is recognition. I see the fire in him—the same
~~~

relentless, unyielding fire that used to burn in me, before the system, in its indifference, had doused it with the cold waters of helplessness.

I stand slowly, leaving the untouched tea behind, a forgotten offering. As I pass his table, our eyes meet again.

I give him a slight nod. Calm. Controlled. A silent challenge. He returns it after a half-second's delay, his brow furrowed in a flicker of confusion.

Then I walk out into the cool, embracing mist of the night. The street breathes around me, exhaling the damp air.

I light the cigarette now, the tip glowing fiercely in the gloom, and take a deep, deliberate drag, watching the smoke curl upwards like a question that will never truly get answered. My phone buzzes in my pocket. A text.

Match confirmed. Kidney delivered. Girl stable.

My lips twitch into a smile. Brief. Contained. A private victory.

One more life saved.

Somewhere in this vast, sprawling city, a child is waking up with a future stitched into her very being. She'll go to school next week. Maybe learn to dance, twirling without pain. Or run for the very first time, her tiny legs pumping with newfound strength. Someone who was utterly out of time... has more now. An extension. A gift.

She'll never know me. That's fine. They don't have to know who I am, or the price paid for their new chance. They just need to live.

I still hear Lily sometimes. In the soft, persistent fall of the rain. In the breathless hush between moments.

"Joe," she calls me, in that quiet, trembling voice I remember so perfectly, "Does it still count if someone had to get hurt so someone else could live?"

I want to say yes. I want to scream it loud enough to silence the crushing weight of guilt that perpetually clings to me.

But instead, I whisper it to myself, the words a silent prayer into the misty night. Again, and again.

"Yes, Lily. It counts."

Because the system doesn't care about people like you. But I do.

~~~

Daniel is digging, and he is sharp enough to find something eventually. Better he finds a thread I've loosely laid than stumble upon something that could truly unravel my entire operation. But my plan to distract him might just work.

However, beyond the practical, there's a... fascination. Daniel represents the system I disdain, yet he embodies the very drive, the very desperation I once felt. He searches for closure, for truth, for justice in a world that often denies it. And in his pursuit, he will inevitably expose more of the cracks, more of the failures of that system. He might not understand my methods, but he will, in his own way, highlight the need for them.

And truthfully? A part of me, the part that still aches for Lily, craves to be seen. To have my reasoning, my ultimate sacrifice, understood, even if it's by an adversary. It's a dangerous impulse, a human weakness I usually suppress. But sometimes, even for a ghost, there's a need to be acknowledged.

A need for the system to see what it failed to do, and what I *did*.
~~~

XVI

Daniel

The cold tea, left untouched on the café table, still bothers me. Its very presence, a silent accusation, gnaws at my mind like a riddle no one has asked. Why order something if you have no intention of drinking it? Why sit two tables away, angled just enough to be seen, to observe without overtly staring? He had nodded. I had nodded back. A fleeting, civil exchange. Forgettable, to anyone else.

But I have a bad feeling about him. Because I am trained to. Because my gut, a seasoned instrument of caution, doesn't stop chewing on the small, incongruous details, not when I am this deep into something I can't yet name. Something is profoundly off with that guy.

If I've learned anything from this city's underbelly, it is that still water often means something is drowning beneath it.

I step outside into the palpable fog. The rain has eased into a fine, clinging mist now, just heavy enough to smear the pavement into a dull blur of reflections, turning the streetlights into hazy halos. The city glows like a distorted memory, out of focus, just out of reach. I trace my steps back toward my car, but the thought of home, of the silent, empty apartment, is unbearable. I need air. Space. Time to think, to let the fragmented pieces swirl and settle.

My phone buzzes, a jolt in the quiet night. It is Jack.

"Hey," I answer, my voice tight.

"Anything?"

"We've got something," he says, his tone grim. "A call from a burner phone."

"Call from who?" My heart hammers against my ribs.

"No voice. Just eleven seconds. Open line. Background noise only."

"Play it."

I press my phone to my ear as static rolls in, a grainy hiss. Then, faintly, indistinct yet utterly clear—a sound. Laughter. A child's laughter. Soft, pure, untainted.

It hits me like a physical blow to the chest, stealing my breath, sharp and agonizing.

"Play that again."

Jack loops it. The sound, impossibly innocent, replays: a little girl laughing. Not screaming. Not crying. Laughing.

"What's the background say?" I demand, my voice raw.

"Audio tech says the reverb matches a public memorial garden near Harbor Street. You know the one—with the statues?"

"Yeah. I'm heading there now."

~~~

The memorial garden is deserted by the time I arrive, swallowed by the mist and the lingering gloom. The iron gate hangs loosely chained, a mere suggestion of a barrier, not truly locked. I slip through, the cold metal scraping faintly against itself.

There is always something profoundly tragic about places meant for remembering children. Sculpted angels,
~~~

their marble faces perpetually mournful. Benches with names carved in cold stone, each one a testament to unbearable loss. Flowers, long since wilted and forgotten, dotting the landscape. They don't just stand there; they scream with a deafening silence.

I follow the winding, gravel path toward the center, guided by the dim glow of my phone's flashlight. It leads to a modest statue of a little girl, frozen in time, holding a delicate paper crane. It is chipped at one wing, a tiny imperfection. At its base, a patch of flattened grass, disturbed by something recent. And there, stark against the damp earth: cigarette ash.

A still-warm cigarette butt, its cherry still glowing faintly in the mist.

Whoever the man from the cafe was, whoever is behind all of this, he has been here. Sat right here, made that anonymous call, leaving just enough of a trace to say: I'm ahead of you. I'm watching.

Why here? Why a memorial garden? My mind races, trying to bridge the gap. Because it means something to him. Or someone.

I crouch, examining the ground around the statue. No distinct shoe prints, the mist too heavy, but a clear, circular smudge—like a thermos or a small jar had been placed here. It is ritualistic.

Measured. Precise.

Like everything else about him.

Who the hell are you?

~~~

I spend the rest of the night lost in a frenetic cross-referencing of medical records. To find something. *Anything.* Perhaps, of a child. For some reason, I began digging through all kinds of possibilities which is exactly
~~~

what makes me look into not just public hospitals, but obscure underground donor registries, shadowy transplant networks, and private clinics that don't ask questions. I call in a favour from a friend in data forensics, pushing the limits of my authority, gaining backdoor access to internal transplant logs.

The patterns begin to emerge, chillingly clear.

Three patients. Three seemingly miraculous, last-minute organ donations. All listed as "unregistered private donor." No next of kin. No matches on official record. Just clean approvals, surgeries greenlit with lightning speed, lives saved.

I compare them to the missing persons reports.

My victims.

Their bodies are never found, only their profound, aching absence. All of them had no trace of trauma, no sign of struggle on the scenes of their disappearances. Just gone.

What if... what if they weren't killed in rage? What if they were meticulously selected?

I lean back in my chair, the sudden stillness of the precinct around me deafening, my pulse ticking like a time bomb. This isn't serial killing in the conventional sense. This is procurement. Structured. Precise. Surgical.

He's harvesting.

The thought makes me recoil, a visceral revulsion. It is barbaric. Inhuman. But as I stare at the printouts scattered across my table, another word, insidious and unsettling, creeps into my mind.

Purposeful.

He isn't selling them. There is no trace of profit, no black-market ring, no surgical waste dumped in clandestine locations, no ransom letters. The organs—kidneys, livers, even hearts—are delivered to hospitals anonymously, always. And the recipients? Always people with no time left. Dying children. Young adults on their last, desperate transplant cycle.

He isn't killing for pleasure. He isn't even killing for revenge, not in the traditional sense.

He is killing... to *save*.

And I hate how that makes a twisted, horrifying sense.

I rub my temple, a dull ache throbbing behind my eyes. I should feel utterly disgusted. Outraged. But instead, I feel... conflicted. A sickening jumble of horror and a perverse understanding.

Then a thought, cold and ugly, strikes me. A slow-moving dread rising from the pit of my stomach, spreading through my veins.

Jessica.

My chest tightens, a vice-like grip stealing my breath. My hands, resting on the damning files, go still, utterly paralyzed.

What if...

No. I couldn't think like that. It isn't justice. It is playing God, a monstrous perversion of medicine.

But what if God isn't watching?

I pin the photo of the memorial garden to my corkboard, a stark, confusing image. And I write a single word beneath it, stark and burning:

Why?

Why does someone become this? Why does someone choose to cross that line—not for money or anger, but to correct the system, to become its brutal, self-appointed surgeon?

He's out there. Watching me. Leaving traces. Not careless. Not cocky.

Deliberate.

He wants to be understood. Maybe even caught.

Or maybe... challenged.

A new, frantic urgency surges through me. I need to check all the files, every single one, to make sure Jess is still out there, that she hasn't become another one of his "donations."

Was she taken?

Was her body one of the ones that simply vanished?

I glance at all the other remaining files. The one detailing the miraculous transplant. A kidney. To a ten-year-old girl. Critical case. Donor: "anonymous." The timing. The timing matches. My throat closes, a dry, burning constriction. Yet, simultaneously, I am filled with an intense urge to scream, to lash out at the universe for its cruel irony.

This was the same day I logged Jess's disappearance.

Is this why he wanted me to know?

He took her. Preserved her. Used her death to give someone else a future.

I drop to my knees, the hard floor unforgiving. I hear myself. Not a whimper, not a cry.

Roaring in fury.

And honestly, I didn't know I had it in me to scream like that.

XVII

Joseph

There's a difference in the air when a man stops searching blindly and starts following a scent. Daniel has caught it. The trace I left for him — the tea, untouched, the phone call from the garden — was enough to divert him. Not too much. Just enough to tickle the back of his mind like a whisper in a locked room.

He'll turn it over in his head a dozen times, replay the angles, the timing, the laughter. That part was a gift. Not a taunt — something deeper. A nudge into memory. Maybe it reminded him of someone. Maybe it hurt.

Good.

Pain sharpens the mind.

I want him sharp. I want him focused. Because even if I tell myself that I do this for the people who deserve to live — for those desperate for second chances — I won't deny it anymore: part of me enjoys this.

The game. The tension. The knowledge that I'm always one step ahead.

Daniel is smart. But I'm careful. I've lived in the blind spots long enough to know where the light never touches.

I sit in a dimly lit room above a laundromat that no one uses anymore, scrolling through the list of names I pulled last week. Suicide forums. Helplines. Support groups.

You'd be amazed how many people are quietly begging for death — and how the world politely ignores them. Clutching platitudes. Prescribing numbness. Pretending grief isn't a hunger with teeth.

And then I see her.

Lana Ward. Twenty-six.

She posted yesterday: "If I die, at least my body might be useful. But I doubt anyone would want it."

I lean back in my chair and stare at her photo. She looks tired. Like someone who's already said goodbye to herself in a hundred small ways.

I pull up her medical file — public insurance, history of mental illness, no family listed. Her organs? Viable. Untouched by addiction. Rare blood type. She could save three lives. Maybe four.

And she wants to die.

The world calls me a killer. I am.

But I'm also a listener.

When people say they want out — truly say it — I believe them.

Lana's cry for help isn't loud, but it's sincere. She's not asking for rescue. She's asking to matter.

And I can give her that. So, I reach out to her.

That evening, I find her waiting outside the pharmacy near 9th Street. She's holding a paper bag filled with antidepressants she won't take. Her eyes scan the sidewalk like she's hoping someone will stop her. No one does.

But I do.

"Rough night?" I ask, softly.

She flinches, surprised I even noticed.

"I guess," she murmurs.

We talk. Ten minutes. Twenty. Her voice cracks only once — when she says, "I don't think I'm built to keep surviving."

And I say, "What if you didn't have to? What if you could make your pain mean something?"

She looks up at me. Confused and a little scared maybe.

I take her to the place no one knows about. The basement in the alley. The room where the air is clean and the metal shines like mercy. She doesn't ask where we are. She doesn't scream. At least not yet.

"I'm not here to convince you to live," I tell her. "But I can give your end a purpose."

She tenses. Her lips tremble. And I know she is changing her mind.

Well, I can't have that now, can I?

I cover her mouth with a cloth and muffle her screams. After a few messed up seconds, I twist her neck in one simple motion.

I hear the thud as her body hits the floor.

I bend near her and whisper thanks.

I prepare her body with care, catalog every usable part, freeze what needs preserving. I pack the boxes with surgical precision, mark the labels, call in the delivery.

Two hospitals. One woman with liver failure. One man on dialysis, father of three.

By morning, both will wake up with a future they didn't have yesterday.

XVIII
Daniel

He killed Jessica.

I keep repeating that like a mantra, a grim prayer, needing the words to stay fresh, sharp, cutting through the fog of exhaustion and disbelief. I can't let myself dull them with doubt, can't allow the horror to soften into something manageable. I've done the math, meticulously, obsessively. The timing. The patient who miraculously received a liver transplant just two days after Jessica vanished. No donor match in any official registry. No family consent documented. Just another file marked "anonymous," a sterile lie in a cold database.

He killed her. My wife.

And now I know what this is. This isn't just about the victims anymore, the growing list of people vanishing into thin air, the weird gaps in hospital records, the blurred, useless footage from street corners. This isn't just a case. It's about revenge. This is personal now, a fire that burns brighter than any oath I ever took.

I've barely slept since I found out. He took her. And he turned her body into inventory, a collection of spare parts.

The thought twisted my gut into a knot of searing pain and righteous fury.

The trace evidence team finally gets back to me on the memorial site. "Cigarette brand is custom rolled," Jack's voice crackles through the phone, sounding tired, but determined. "Tobacco from a niche supplier in West Briar. Only about fifty registered clients in the area. We're narrowing it."

"Good," I bite out, my voice raw. "I want names, deliveries, payment trails. Get a warrant if you must. I don't care about red tape now."

He hesitates. "Dan, we don't even have a face yet. No ID, no prints. He's careful, too careful."

"I don't care how careful he is," I growl, the anger a hot, corrosive bile in my throat. "We catch him. Period."

He sighs, a sound of weary resignation. "I'll keep pushing."

I don't thank him. I just hang up, the sharp click of the phone final. I don't have the luxury of gratitude right now, only the gnawing hunger for retribution.

I open a new, pristine folder on my case board, its white surface stark against the chaos of my notes. Lana Ward. Twenty-six. History of depression. No family. Reported missing just last night. The timestamp on her last known location places her outside a pharmacy on 9th Street. She never picks up her prescription.

I know it is him. A cold, certain dread settles over me. It is the kind of victim he chooses—vulnerable, alone, invisible to most. But not to him.

I scan the city camera feeds near 9th Street, pulling up the grainy black-and-white footage, my eyes burning from lack of sleep. At 7:46 p.m., Lana steps outside the pharmacy, clutching a small paper bag. She hesitates, a tiny, almost imperceptible shift of weight, as if waiting for something. Then, a man approaches. He is a shadow, wearing a hood pulled low, his face obscured by the darkness and the poor resolution. They talk. Lana nods. At 7:59 p.m., they disappear down a side street that has no camera coverage.

Gone. Just like that.

I punch the wall beside the corkboard, a dull thud resonating through the precinct. Not because it helps, but because I need to feel something physical, something real, to drown out the inferno behind my eyes, the screaming rage that threatens to consume me. She's gone. Just like the others. And he'll preserve her like meat in a market. Label her organs. Package them like salvation. And someone—somewhere—will get to live.

But that doesn't make him a hero. It makes him a killer. And I'm going to bring him down.

Jack calls back two hours later; his voice clipped with urgency. "We got something. One of the tobacco clients is a guy named Neil Harwood. Lives above a closed-down laundromat in East Briar. No criminal record. Paid in cash. No digital footprint in five years."

East Briar. My mind instantly pulls up the city grid. That's close to the delivery hub where one of the anonymous donor shipments came through last month. Right in the middle of a transportation dead zone—no cameras, no license plates logged, a perfect blind spot.

"I want eyes on him now," I bark, my voice low and dangerous. "Surveillance. Plainclothes only. Don't spook him. Do not spook him."

"What if he's not our guy?" Jack asks, a hint of caution in his voice.

"Well, what if he is?" I shoot back. He doesn't argue.

That night, I drive by Harwood's building myself. I park two blocks away, kill the engine, and sit in the suffocating silence of my patrol car, my hand resting on the cool, reassuring weight of my sidearm. The windows are dark, anonymous squares against the brick façade. But I see movement behind a curtain, a flicker of shadow. A faint pulse of light, gone as quickly as it appears.

He's in there. I think about kicking the door in right now. Dragging him into the street. Making him feel everything he stole from me, every agonizing second of my grief.

But he doesn't look like a killer in any way, not from the brief, distorted glimpse I'd seen. Neil Harwood. A mundane name for a monstrous deed. Maybe Jack is right. I need to focus. To think straight. Not to act on blind fury. I want this clean. Ironclad. No way out for him. I want the killer in a box, irrevocably trapped.

It is storming when I finally get home, the thunder rolling low and guttural, like the city itself is growling, mirroring the turmoil in my soul. I strip off my soaked jacket, the chill clinging to my skin, and stare at the case board again.

Victims. Timelines. Medical files. Transplant recipients. Their smiling faces in news articles, beaming with newfound life: "Young woman saved by miracle donor," "Father of three gets a second chance at life." And all I see is the cost.

You don't get to call yourself a saviour if you kill people in the dark. You don't get to decide who dies, even if someone else gets to live. He didn't ask. He didn't explain. He just took her. And that, more than anything else, is what seals this for me, solidifying my resolve into a concrete slab of vengeance.

He made himself God. And now he's going to answer to a man who knows what it's like to be left behind, a man who knows the agony of loss he so casually inflicts.

I go back to the couch and pull out my service weapon, its cold steel familiar in my hands. I begin to clean it, slowly, methodically, wiping away invisible dust, polishing the cold metal, the way he probably sterilizes his scalpels. The difference is: mine will be used for justice. His—for murder.

And I don't care how many lungs or livers he delivers, wrapped in good intentions. I'm coming for him. And when I find him, no hospital, no grateful family he's "helped," no twisted excuse will protect him.

XIX

Joseph

Mr. Whiskers curls beside me, a warm, purring ballast against the tumultuous seas of my thoughts. He is a quiet ball of tabby fur, the only living thing in this desolate apartment that doesn't demand explanations, doesn't ask questions I can't answer. He flicks his tail against my thigh, a steady, unbothered metronome ticking out time. He doesn't know the things I've done. Or perhaps he does, and simply doesn't care, content in his feline apathy.

The cool, ethereal glow from the television paints the room in flickering gold, dancing across the worn furniture, illuminating dust motes in the stagnant air. I don't normally indulge in old recordings, don't often allow myself to journey back to the shattered fragments of my past. But tonight... tonight is different. Tonight, the dam has broken.

The video plays on the screen, a grainy little box of time preserved by accident and sentiment. There we are: me, all gangly limbs and awkward angles, maybe seventeen; Lily, seven years younger, a tiny whirlwind of skinny limbs and toothy, gap-filled grins. We are in the backyard of the house

I prefer not to remember, a place haunted by spectres of normalcy. I am holding a neon green water gun, its plastic barrel glinting. She is shrieking, a sound that is half delighted laughter, half mock-threat of revenge, as she darts behind the ancient oak tree. "Come out, Lily!" I call after her, my voice carrying easily across the sun-drenched lawn. "You're not that sneaky!"

Her tiny voice squeals back, brimming with pure, unadulterated joy. "I'm invisible!"

And I laugh.

God, that sound. My own laughter. Unrestrained. Young. Whole. It is the most honest version of me that has ever existed—the me before everything shattered, before the world showed its cruel, indifferent face.

The screen blurs, and not because of the video quality. My vision swims, but I don't bother to wipe my eyes. Mr. Whiskers meows softly, a gentle, understanding rumble, and presses a soft paw against my wrist as if he knows the precise agony of that moment. I scratch behind his ear, feeling the soft, warm fur.

"I know, buddy," I whisper, my voice thick.

The camera shakes violently in the video, a dizzying shift as we switch scenes. Lily is holding the camera now, pointing it precariously at me as I read something dramatically from a worn, leather-bound book, pretending to be a menacing villain. Her giggles snort through the tinny speaker, little bursts of pure delight. She zooms in too close on my face, blurring my features, and I shout, "Too much! You're going to break it!" She just laughs harder, her small body shaking with mirth.

They left us when she got sick. Our parents.

You'd think it would've been the other way around—that tragedy draws people closer, forging bonds of shared suffering. But not them. When the doctors first utter the words "Lily's heart," when they explain that she'd need endless tests, gruelling treatments, and eventually, a transplant, they look at each other like two investors watching a stock crash, their faces devoid of emotion, only calculation.

They weren't built for sacrifice. They were built for spreadsheets and silence. For tidy columns and balanced ledgers. They cashed in life insurance policies, liquidated every conceivable asset, and left town before the first wave of medical bills even started arriving. I was legally adult, barely, but old enough to be legally responsible, and irrevocably, devastatingly, legally abandoned.

Lily was eight. And so, so scared.

I remember the night she cried into my shoulder, her small body trembling, her breath hitching like a skipping tape recorder. She asks, her voice barely a whisper, "Is it something I did? Is that why they don't love me?"

I don't have an answer that isn't a lie. "They do love you," I'd said, my voice cracking. "They're just... confused. Lost. But I'm not. I'm here. Always."

And I was.

I took her to every appointment, memorizing the sterile corridors, the detached faces of specialists. I learned to cook with low-sodium ingredients, transforming our kitchen into a pharmacy of bland necessity. I learned what medications interacted badly, the subtle signs of a dangerous cocktail. I held her hair when she threw up, my own stomach churning in sympathy. I bought her stargazing books, worn and dog-eared, and sat with her on the cold roof even when it was freezing, because she loved naming constellations. She said it made her feel like she belonged to something bigger, something grander than her failing heart.

I was her brother. And her father. And her entire, fragile world. And she was mine.

The video shifts again, a static jump. She is at the old upright piano, playing something soft and simple, a children's lullaby. Her fingers are thin and precise, dancing over the yellowed keys, her hair a charming mess. I am in the corner of the frame, pretending not to cry, my face carefully blank, because I know what is coming—the next appointment, the next terrifying scan. The next "sorry, there's nothing more we can do."

Her condition deteriorated quickly, brutally. Her heart grew weaker with every passing week, a drum fading into a whisper. The doctors finally said she needed a transplant then, but no donor was available. She was too small. Too rare. Too forgotten by a system that simply didn't work fast enough for people who mattered too little. I begged. I pleaded. I screamed at closed doors, offered to pay anything, everything, but we were too far gone by then. We had no connections. No leverage. No one to pull strings. We were just two kids lost in the immense, uncaring cracks of the world.

The last week of her life, she could barely sit up. I remembered spoon-feeding her mashed fruit, soft and bland, while she watched her favourite cartoon on mute. Not because the sound bothered her—but because she didn't want to hear what she couldn't laugh at anymore.

She died while I was making her favourite chamomile tea. One minute, I was boiling water, the kettle whistling its mundane tune. The next, the monitor beside her bed flatlined. Quiet. No alarms. Just... stopped. And my world went with her, collapsing into silent, suffocating dust.

People talk about grief like it's fire or ice, a burning inferno or a freezing desolation. For me, it is water. It fills me, seeps into every part of me, makes everything heavy and slow. It drowns my logic, my patience, every shred of hope. And when I finally surface for air, gasping and broken, I'm not the same. I'm not Joseph anymore. I am the echo of what Lily left behind. A blueprint made of loss, drawn in the deepest shadows of despair.

That night, consumed by a raw, primal anguish, I stood at the edge of the city bridge and stared at the churning black water below, wondering if I should simply join her, escape the unbearable weight of existence. But then, an image flashed in my mind: the children who were still waiting in hospital beds, their faces pale, their breaths shallow. The mothers who still prayed nightly, clutching worn rosaries. The lovers gripping the hands of partners too weak to grip back, their eyes filled with silent pleas.

And I realized something cold and clear, a truth that cut through the fog of grief:

The system wasn't broken.

It was designed to fail.

It was designed to favour paperwork over people, insurance codes over survival. It waited too long. It moved too slow. It calculated risk while people rotted in hospital beds, their futures dissolving into the sterile air.

But I could move faster. I could choose.

So, I did.

The first was a man I found on a suicide forum, a ghost haunting the digital landscape. He'd tried three times already; each attempt a desperate cry for release. He had no family, no connections, no one to mourn his passing. He begged for someone to end it, to give him peace. I met him in a desolate parking lot, the night air heavy with unspoken despair, and asked him one question: "Do you want your death to mean something?"

He cried, silent tears tracking paths through the grime on his face. But he was the first and the last to ever accept it willingly. The only victim of mine who agreed to be killed, who desperately wanted to at least be of use after his death. I gave him a quick and painless end, a merciful finality since he didn't fight me, didn't even flinch.

And his liver saved a boy in a hospital I used to walk Lily past on good days, a bright, cheerful building that once held a fleeting promise.

I never looked back. I didn't need to.

People asked themselves all kinds of questions when they did something terrible. Was I still a good person? Would anyone forgive me? I didn't ask those things. Because I didn't regret it. Not one donor. Not one night. Not one life taken in place of another.

I am not a monster.

I am a *correction*.

I am what happens when the world let people like Lily die quietly, forgotten, and expects no one to answer for it. Well, I answered. And I kept answering.

The video ends. The screen fades to black, a mirror reflecting my own haunted face. Mr. Whiskers nuzzles my elbow and lets out a long, slow sigh, as if even he feels the immense weight of the silence.

I press the remote. Replay.

Lily's laughter floods the room again, vibrant and pure, a beacon in the darkness. I smile. Not the smile of peace, not quite. But the smile of someone who has made peace with war.

XX
Daniel

I never gave her a funeral. Not really.

There was no body. No casket. Just a closed case file, a hushed whisper from the medical examiner, a cold, clinical signature on a death certificate that answered absolutely nothing. We cremate an empty shell—a guess, a desperate act of faith—and call it grief. I dress in black, a stark, lifeless silhouette in a sea of well-meaning faces. I accept the casseroles, each dish a testament to unspoken sympathy. I shake hands and mumble thanks to people whose names and faces blur into an indistinct canvas of sorrow. Before, I never gave her a goodbye. Not one that matters. Not one that truly counts. Because, in my deepest, most guarded heart, I didn't believe she was truly gone.

And now I know why. He took her. He took her body. Her organs. Her name. Her peace. And left me nothing but a gaping, bleeding void.

So today... I don't bury her. But I still say goodbye.

~~~

The memorial is small—just me, a simple, empty urn, and the worn photo album she loved, its pages filled with
~~~

laughter and sunlight. I stand by the river near our old bench, the willow tree weeping silently beside us, its long branches swaying like a gentle benediction. I scatter dried flowers onto the shimmering surface of the water, each fragile petal a promise I never get to keep, a silent apology for my failure. Her scarf, soft and familiar, is wrapped tightly around my wrist, catching the breeze like a phantom hand reaching back, a final, tender touch.

There is no priest. No mournful music. Just the profound silence of the morning, broken only by the gentle lapping of the river against its banks. And her name, a whispered prayer, hanging in the cool, humid air.

"Jessica," I whisper, my voice raw, breaking on the syllables. "You were my home."

~~~

I close my eyes, and suddenly, she is there. Her smile. God, that smile—tilted, sly, the kind that makes me feel like she is in on some secret the world hasn't quite figured out yet. It is a conspiratorial curve of her lips, a spark in her eyes that promises adventure and mischief.

I remember our first date. A quirky bookstore café, the air thick with the scent of old paper and roasted coffee. She walks in wearing her favorite blue-colored coat, vibrant against the muted tones of the room, holding a cup of coffee like it is a weapon, ready to take on the day. She sits across from me, her eyes twinkling, and says, "You have the most suspicious eyebrows I've ever seen." I laugh. Not a chuckle, but a full, uninhibited roar that lasts for ten straight minutes, drawing curious glances from other patrons. By the end of that night, I am already in love. Utterly, irrevocably.

We don't have one of those dramatic, tempestuous relationships. No screaming matches that end in slammed
~~~

doors, no passionate makeups in the pouring rain. It is quiet. Solid. Built like a house with thick, enduring walls and big, welcoming windows that let in all the light. We fight, sure. About bills, mundane and frustrating. About what questionable concoction to cook for dinner. About whether or not I leave the toothpaste cap off on purpose, an enduring, silly battle. But mostly, we laugh.

I remember our honeymoon in Florence. She takes three hundred pictures of every single alleyway, convinced each cobblestone and peeling fresco holds a secret love story. "Even the cracks here are romantic," she declares, her eyes wide with wonder. She used to sleep with one foot sticking out from under the blanket, a small rebellion against the covers. She snores softly when she is drunk, a faint, adorable rumble. She dances while brushing her teeth, a silent, joyful rhythm to start each day. She makes everything lighter. Including me.

I don't know you could miss someone in your bones. That you could ache in places you didn't even know existed, a phantom pain in the very marrow of your being. But I do. I miss the way she smells like old books and clean laundry, a comforting, unique scent. I miss the way she says my name when she is mad, the syllables clipped and sharp yet still endearing. I miss the way she would gently touch my face when I am quiet for too long, a silent inquiry. I miss the silence with her—the good kind, the profound, comfortable quiet that never needed filling. I miss being known. Truly, completely known.

~~~

After the quiet memorial, I sit in my car, the interior still and cold, and pull out the photo album I haven't touched since the week she died. It still smells like her—a faint trace of her favourite perfume, mingled with the sweet, spicy
~~~

scent of cinnamon gum. The first picture is from our wedding. Her in that vintage lace dress, luminous and timeless, her hair pinned up with fresh flowers, laughing like the world couldn't possibly touch her. Me in a too-tight suit, looking at her like I couldn't believe I was this lucky, this blessed.

God, I was lucky.

We didn't have everything. No grand fortune, no sprawling estate. But we had enough. We had lazy Saturdays with stacks of pancakes and obscure documentaries. We had spontaneous road trips where we got lost on purpose, just to see where the road would take us. We had stupid traditions, like making each other themed playlists every year on our anniversary, filled with songs that only we understood.

We had each other.

And now, I have this box of photographs and a room in my apartment that still smells faintly of her shampoo, a constant, agonizing reminder.

I thought I'd feel better knowing what happened. I don't. I feel hollow. Like someone ripped out the very part of me that was alive, vibrant, connected, and left the rest to rot, a husk of a man.

He killed her. He saw her as a donor. An opportunity. A match on a spreadsheet. Not a person. Not my wife. He didn't know about the way she cried when dogs died in movies, her empathy boundless. Or how she snorted when she laughed too hard, a charming imperfection. Or how she always bought two coffees—one for herself and one for the barista, just in case they were having a rough day. He didn't know her. But he took her anyway. And now some stranger walks around with her heart beating in their chest.

That should mean something. Something profound. But all it means to me is that Jessica died on a cold, sterile table, alone, while I was miles away, oblivious.

I visit our old spot in the park that afternoon. The weathered wooden bench near the ancient willow tree where we used to bring lunch on Sundays. She used to sit cross-legged, quoting poetry she didn't really understand, her brow furrowed in mock concentration. I'd tease her about it, and she'd roll her eyes, then lean over and kiss me just to shut me up.

I sit there now, hands shoved deep in my coat pockets, staring at the empty space beside me, a gaping hole where she should have been. "You'd think I'd have something profound to say," I murmur to the empty air, the words catching in my throat. "But I don't." I pause, listening to the rustle of leaves. "I just miss you. So damn much."

A gentle breeze brushes past me, light and soft, carrying the scent of damp earth and distant rain. It almost feels like her.

~~~

There are days I want to quit. To give it all up, disappear somewhere far away, drown myself in memories and whiskey, and simply wait for the pain to dull, to numb into oblivion. But then I remember the man who did this. The man who chose her. Who looked at my wife—my life, my entire world—and saw nothing but utility. An organ. A solution to someone else's tragedy.

He plays God in basements and back alleys and actually believes it's noble. But I don't give a damn how many lungs or livers he delivers, wrapped in his twisted, self-righteous intentions.

He took Jessica. And I'm going to make sure he answers for it.
~~~

Still, today... today is for her. Not for vengeance. Not for anger. Just for love.

I pull out the last photo in the album. It isn't fancy. Just a blurry selfie she took of us lying on the couch, half-asleep, my arm a loose cradle around her, her smile soft and sleepy, utterly content. She had titled it, simply, "Home." It was the last time I felt truly safe.

The sun begins to set, slow and deliberate, painting the sky in hues of orange and purple, turning everything gold—like a painting she would have loved, would have photographed a hundred times. I close the album, its worn cover cool against my trembling hands, and rest it on my lap.

"I love you," I whisper to the fading light. "I don't know who I am without you."

I wait, a foolish hope flaring, like maybe she'd answer, a faint whisper on the wind. She doesn't. But the wind moves gently through the trees, a soft sigh, and for a second, it feels like maybe she's still here. Watching. Waiting.

And when this is over—when I've hunted him down and looked him in the eyes and shown him what grief truly is—maybe then I'll let go.

But not just yet.

XXI

Joseph

He's hunting me.

I can feel it. Like breath on the back of my neck. Like thunder too far to hear but close enough to feel in your chest. The distraction I set up won't hold him forever. He'll eventually see through it.

Daniel is not chasing a theory anymore — he's chasing me. And not blindly. No, he's methodical. Furious, yes, but focused.

There's something about being pursued by someone who is relentless. And that, I admit, excites me.

But more than the fear of getting caught, it's the excitement of being *known* that dominates. Plus of course, the *fun*.

Mr. Whiskers is curled in my lap as I sit on the floor of my apartment. No lights. Just the soft, flickering grey of a paused video on the television screen. Lily's smile is frozen mid-laugh — that perfect, glowing laugh she had when I used to chase her around the backyard with a garden hose. She had no idea what would come later. No idea that the world she was dancing through was counting down the days she had left.

I keep the video paused like that often. Like it keeps her alive, just a little longer.

My hand strokes Mr. Whiskers absentmindedly. He purrs like thunder under my palm, completely unbothered by the storm building outside this apartment. He's the only living thing that has ever stayed.

I remember the way Lily used to hold him — before he was mine, when he was just a tiny little kitten, only a few days old. He belonged to her first. She called him Captain Meow. He hated the name, but he loved her. We both did.

And now, he's the only witness left to everything I've become.

But now my attention goes to my laptop screen, where I get a pop-up.

Tasha sent me an email three weeks ago. Her subject line was simple:

"Can my pain serve a purpose?"

She didn't plead. She didn't beg for a saviour. She simply asked to matter.

Stage IV cancer. Terminal. Morphine dependency. Alone. No family. No debts. Nothing left but a calendar of palliative reminders and a body that aches when she breathes.

We met twice. Once in a bookstore café, where she told me how she used to be a teacher. How she loved children. How she hated that her bones felt like ash now. The second time was here — in this apartment — where she saw Lily's photo on the wall and cried for someone she never knew.

I told her the truth. I always do.

I told her what I do. How it works. How it ends.

I also told her this — that her cancer had already taken what donation usually requires. That her organs could not be used.

But not everything was lost.

Her eyes could still give sight. Her skin could still heal burns. Her tissues could still ease pain, restore movement, give someone else time.

Even now, even like this, parts of her could still matter.

And she said yes.

Not because she wanted to die — but because she didn't want to keep surviving for nothing.

Finally, someone who is willingly ready to do this after a very long time.

Well, if there's a first, there always will be a second.

At exactly 6:00 p.m., she arrives at the address I gave her. Right on time.

She wears a clean shirt, plain jeans. No makeup. Her hair is wrapped in a scarf patterned with yellow sunflowers. "I wanted to look nice," she says softly. "For them."

For the people she's going to save.

I nod. "You do."

We talk for a while — I let her lead the conversation. We drink tea. She asks about Lily. I tell her about the hospital roof, the stars, the books she used to annotate with glitter pens. Tasha smiles through tears.

"She must've been beautiful," she says.

"She was everything."

I take her to the alley when she's ready.

The basement is sterile, yes. But not cold. I've made sure of that. There's warmth in the lights, a chair beside the table, a framed picture on the far wall of a tree blooming in spring.

She lies down without fear.

No straps. No force.

I explain every step.

She leaves behind a note for the recipients. She doesn't want them to know her name, only that she was proud to help.

The sedation is gentle. Her breathing slows like a whisper. Her fingers remain curled around the sunflower scarf.

She doesn't cry.

Neither do I.

It's her choice. And I am barely helping her to do it right.

I work with practiced grace.

This is not violence.

This is purpose.

Everything is done cleanly, respectfully. Her lungs are perfect. Her liver strong. Even in death, she is generous.

When it's done, I catalog everything. Pack the cooler. Log the temperature.

The driver arrives at midnight — a woman named Hannah, a nurse from the hospital John works at. She doesn't ask questions. Just takes the container and leaves.

By the time she reaches the hospital, a boy who hasn't laughed in two years will have the breath to do so again.

Tasha did that.

Not me.

I was just the vessel.

I sit back in my chair and close my eyes.

I should feel tired.

Instead, I feel... whole.

This is the only time I ever feel close to Lily now — when I know, absolutely, that someone else gets to live because I refused to let the system keep failing.

I look at the surgical table. The floor is clean. Everything disposed of. No evidence.

But I have a feeling that he'll find this place.

Eventually.

And when he does, I want him to know I was here. Not hiding. Not afraid. Just... ahead.

Not to taunt.

To challenge.

He deserves that much.

I step outside into the cool night. The city lights blink like tired stars, and the streets are mostly empty. Just a late-night jogger here. A couple arguing in hushed tones there.

I take the long way to the bridge; the one Lily and I used to sit beneath when she was well enough to walk. She believed in wishes. Tossed pennies like they were promises. Her last wish was that I wouldn't be alone.

I smile at the memory.

"I'm not alone," I murmur. "I've got work. And a cat."

I lean against the rail and stare down into the black ripple of the water.

Somewhere beneath this surface, the old Joseph died.

The one who waited for phone calls from organ banks. The one who prayed and hoped and begged.

The one who thought the world would fix itself if you just believed hard enough.

Well, what do you know?

I didn't wait for some hero to swoop in and save the day.

I was destined to take this path.

Someone had to.

XXII

Daniel

The files lay scattered across my dining table like the fractured pieces of a shattered soul. Names. Photos. Autopsy reports that never happened. Audio transcripts from frantic, unheard calls. Witness testimonials that amounted to little more than whispers into the void. Every fragment cataloged, every fact laid bare, yet still, they remained... just ghosts. And no bodies. Just closed cases, quiet funerals that offered no true peace, unanswered questions that clawed at my insides.

All of them, every single one, had been officially ruled out as unrelated incidents. Vanishings. Maybe suicides. Maybe escapes from lives they couldn't bear. But I have been through every one of these files over the last month, a man drowning in paperwork, consumed by an obsession that wouldn't let me breathe. And now, finally, I see what no one else wanted to.

It wasn't random. It was surgical.

~~~

I stare at the file of a man, twenty-nine, last seen outside a rehab clinic. A recovering opioid addict, two brutal
~~~

relapses scarring his past. His final post on a personal blog, chilling in its quiet despair: "I don't know if I can keep trying. If I'm not here tomorrow, I hope someone understands." I mark the file: High-Risk Suicidal.

Next, a woman, thirty-five. Chronic depression, divorced, two documented suicide attempts. Her sister, her voice flat with exhaustion, tells me, "She talked about dying like it was a vacation she couldn't afford."

Again, High-Risk Suicidal.

The final victim, Tasha. Terminal cancer. Alone. Her doctor's testimonial, a clinical observation of profound resignation: "She told me she wanted control over her own death, and that she didn't want to go slowly."

High-Risk. Terminal. Voluntary Euthanasia Suspected.

I keep going, file after file, the pattern repeating itself like a grim, relentless rhythm. None of them are stable. None of them are screaming, truly begging for rescue. In their own ways, they have already left, their spirits having departed long before their bodies. Some left notes. Some have locked journals filled with their final thoughts. Some left nothing but silence and fading medication prescriptions, a testament to their quiet surrender. But one chilling detail binds them all together: each is in a place where death feels like the next, logical, inevitable step.

Until I get to Jessica.

My hands shake as I open her file, the paper rustling like dry leaves. Even now, it feels wrong, a desecration. Like I am dissecting a precious dream, searching for proof that it isn't real, that she isn't truly gone. She wasn't suicidal. She wasn't depressed. She was... Jessica. Full of warmth, vibrant laughter, stubborn opinions about obscure coffee brands and deliberately mismatched socks. There is no journal. No therapist's notes hinting at despair. No last letter. She just vanished.

And days later, her heart, a beating testament to life, saves a patient in critical failure. An anonymous donor. Just like the others.

I want to scream, to lash out at the injustice, to tear the very fabric of the world. But I hold it in, the rage coiling tighter in my gut.

I hit the streets again, my steps fuelled by a desperate need for answers. I spend the next three days revisiting every name in those damning files. Friends. Roommates. Parents. Doctors. I ask the same questions, twisting them slightly, trying to find a crack in their grief, a hint I'd missed.

"When did you last speak to them?"

"Did they talk about dying?"

"Did anything feel... final?"

And again and again, I get the same answers. Yes. Yes. God, yes. They were fading. Losing light. Pulling away from the people and places they once loved. No one wanted them gone—but no one was truly surprised either.

On the fifth day, I sit in my car outside Jessica's favourite flower shop, its vibrant window displays a stark contrast to the gray despair within me. She used to buy orchids from here every other Sunday, delicate, exotic blooms. She told me they were "moody, like her." I stare through the windshield, letting the silence pour in, the hum of the city fading into a distant drone.

Everyone else on this list was chosen because they wanted out. So why was Jessica taken? What did he see in her, my vibrant, stubborn Jessica?

What made him put her on the table?

I drive home, the questions burning, and tear through every inch of the apartment. Her notebooks, her laptop, her old journals, stacked neatly on her desk, untouched since... Everything she left behind. I find nothing to indicate despair. Although, I do find one folder tucked away in her documents, buried under layers of junk PDFs and forgotten recipes. Inside, pamphlets and files on adoption.

I stare at it, the innocuous papers suddenly heavy with unspoken meaning. Adoption? We'd always talked about having kids, casually, someday. We'd also discussed these other options, the conversations light, hypothetical. My breath catches in my throat. She wanted to start a family. The realization hits me with a fresh wave of pain, an aching tenderness for a future that will never be. Why had she never said anything to me? The files scattered across the table, a chaotic mess, pulling me back to the cold, undeniable facts of the case.

If his pattern is real—if he only chooses those who wanted to die—then Jessica doesn't belong on that list. She was happy. She had plans, dreams of a family, of a future. She didn't qualify.

So, what the hell happened? Was it opportunistic? Did he simply get it wrong, a miscalculation in his twisted benevolence? Or... did he not care?

That's the part that makes my blood run cold, chilling me to the bone. He's precise. Controlled. Intentional. But what if he let that slip? What if her death was the first time he got curious, the first deviation from his monstrous mission statement?

I clench my fists until my nails bite into my palms, the sharp pain a welcome distraction from the spiralling thoughts. I stare at the names on the board again. Victims. Transplants. Hospital recipients. All the puzzle pieces finally begin to snap into place, forming a horrifying, coherent image.

He's not a sadist. He's not a thrill killer. He's a selector. A gatekeeper. And he's harvesting people on the edge, those who have already chosen to surrender. Taking their consent—spoken or not—and turning it into someone else's salvation.

Except Jessica. She breaks the pattern. Which means either I'm missing something, some crucial piece of her final days... Or this bastard chose to break it.

~~~

I drive out to the last known location of one of the earlier victims, Megan. She'd disappeared days before Jessica, a ghost haunting the quiet streets. Her roommate and friend, a nervous, jumpy young woman, named Paige, who came by the precinct when she went missing, tells me during our conversation, "Like I said the other day, she called me the night she disappeared. She said she wanted to end it. I tried talking to her, begging her to come back. She never did. She also gave me her cat. Said her cat didn't deserve to go through more sadness. I'm allergic to cats, so I gave it to one of my other friends, Hannah."

That cat, a tiny, silent witness, I learn, now lives with a nurse named Hannah. I track her down, finding her address through police databases.

Hannah works at a hospital outside the city, a large, modern complex. When I show her my badge, she flinches, not with guilt, but with a flicker of recognition, a subtle shift in her guarded eyes. I watch her carefully as I speak, my voice low and even. "I'm investigating a string of disappearances. Organ donors that never registered. One of the victims gave you her cat, didn't she?"

She nods slowly, her gaze dropping to the floor. "Megan. She was... kind."

"Did you see her after that?"
~~~

"No," she mumbles, but her eyes dart away, a tell-tale sign. I pause, letting the silence hang heavy, knowing she is hiding something. I nod, a silent acknowledgment, and she, relieved, closes the door. I leave for now, but if my suspicion is right, I am closer to finding him. I call Officer Bell, asking him to keep a discreet eye on Hannah, just in case.

At least, I know exactly what kind of man I am chasing now. Someone who sees himself as a saviour. Someone who thinks purpose justifies execution. Someone who turned my wife into his error, his deliberate deviation.

It is dark by the time I get back to the precinct, the city lights blurring through the rain-streaked windshield. I pin the last photo to the board. Not of a victim. But of a man, blurry, grainy, walking away from a camera, head down, his coat flapping in the wind.

But familiar.

I don't have a name yet. But I have motive. The evidence is circumstantial, a web of conjecture and unsettling patterns. But my rage is not. It is real. Tangible. Fuelling every beat of my exhausted heart.

I sit at my desk and close my eyes, the harsh fluorescent lights of the precinct doing little to dispel the shadows in my mind. I see Jessica's smile, vibrant and full of life. The way she used to hold her coffee with both hands, like it was too precious to spill. The way she smelled like lavender and rain, a scent that still clings to my clothes. I see the ring on her finger, the simple gold band that is a testament to our vows. The worn blanket on our couch, imprinted with the countless hours we'd spent curled up together. The damn playlist she left on my phone, a cruel symphony of our shared past that I still can't listen to without breaking.

And I see him. Whoever he is. The man who looked at her life and saw it as optional.

I whisper, the words a fierce vow into the quiet emptiness of the room, "I will find you." I promise it. Not just because I'm a cop, bound by duty and the law. But because I'm her husband, bound by love and a thirst for vengeance.

XXIII

Joseph

The call comes just after 1 a.m. I'm feeding Mr. Whiskers—or rather, watching him meticulously devour his kibble—when my phone buzzes, vibrating once, then twice, a sharp, insistent tremor on the cool countertop beside the sink. My eyes flicker to the screen: JOHN. He isn't one for casual conversation, especially not in the dead of night.

I swipe to answer, my voice already tight with anticipation. "Talk."

"There's a kid. Thirteen years old," John's voice crackles through the line, clipped and urgent. "Kidney failure. Type AB-negative. We've tried five registries. Nothing. Too rare. She's crashing, Joseph."

My grip tightens on the phone. "How long?"

"Eight hours, max. Maybe less. Dialysis is failing. Doctors are prepping her for surgery in case a miracle falls out of the sky."

I close my eyes, already calculating, running the silent algorithms in my mind. *AB-negative.* Rare. A bottleneck in the desperate, endless demand for life. But not impossible.

"I might have something," I say, my voice low, controlled. "Let me check the archive."

A pause stretches between us, thick with unspoken hope. "You sure?" John's voice holds a tremor of disbelief.

"No. But I'm not out of luck yet."

John exhales; relief barely disguised beneath the urgent edge of his tone. "I owe you."

"You already do." I hang up, the click of the phone final, severing the connection.

Mr. Whiskers looks up at me, his emerald eyes unblinking, as if he knows exactly where I'm going, what I'm about to do. Like he always knows. "Stay out of trouble," I murmur, scratching behind his ears. He twitches one ear, a small acknowledgment, then returns to his meal, purring contentedly.

~~~

The city is quiet as I drive, a muted symphony of distant hums and the soft shush of my tires on the wet asphalt. It's one of those post-rain nights where the roads shine like polished obsidian, every surface reflecting the golden glow of streetlights, blurring them into half-melted gold. The air is crisp, clean, washed free of the day's grime. No one watches me. No one follows. I am just another shadow, another phantom moving through the dark, nothing out of place in this indifferent metropolis. Good. That's exactly how I like it.

I reach the alley behind Sycamore Street just after 1:30 a.m. It has been shut down for years, the brick facades crumbling, windows boarded up like vacant eyes. No electricity runs to the building, not officially, but I've rerouted that long ago, a private power line humming in the silence. I slip through the rusted gate, the creak barely audible, and descend the narrow, winding staircase that
~~~

leads to my subterranean lab.

The heavy steel door at the bottom groans in protest as I push it open, revealing the familiar sanctuary within. The basement smells of bleach and cold metal—sharp, sterile, immaculately clean. Exactly the way I left it.

The storage units hum in the silence, a low, constant vibration. Ten upright freezers stand against the far wall; each one marked with a coded label. I keep them meticulously organized by blood type, condition, and viability window. It is essential. There is absolutely no room for error, no space for mistakes down here.

I cross to Unit AB, my fingers steady as I type in the code. The seal releases with a soft hiss of chilled air, a frosty breath against my face. Inside, nestled on gleaming racks, are five carefully preserved bags. Stabilized. Tracked. Ready.

I take the thick logbook from the shelf beside the freezer and flick to the AB-negative entries. Two kidneys are listed. One from a man in his early forties; too large for a child, and a slight tissue mismatch. The second—female, twenty, no genetic anomalies. Bloodwork stable. Perfect tissue profile. Candidate viable.

I pull the bag carefully from the rack, its surface opaque with frost, and inspect it beneath the harsh lab light. No clouding. No breakdown. Fully frozen, but ready for rapid thaw. She is going to make it.

I place the organ into the portable preservation chamber I've meticulously designed and built myself, a marvel of quiet efficiency, and initiate the thawing cycle. The machine hisses softly, a mechanical breath as cold air circulates in precise, regulated bursts. Fifteen minutes. That's all the time I have to prepare it, to bring it back to a state of fragile readiness.

I text John, my fingers flying across the screen: "Found the match. Delivering within the hour. Prep your OR."

He replies instantly, a single word of profound gratitude: "Bless you."

But I don't need blessings. I need results. This is what I do—not out of kindness, not for redemption, not for gratitude. I do it because the system couldn't. Because no one else would. Because Lily died waiting. And this girl tonight won't.

~~~

As the thawing unit hums its quiet, mechanical tune, I turn to the old, unassuming cabinet in the back corner. Inside are the files—old, yellowing paper files from the earliest days, when I still kept names. Before I realized names were dangerous. Before I learned how hope, if you said it out loud, too loudly, too often, turned into a liability.

I pull one out, its edges soft with age. L. Marsh. Nineteen. Severe PTSD. Attempted suicide twice. Left a note, scrawled in a shaky hand: "Don't waste me. Use me." Her kidney saved a four-year-old boy, giving him a future he'd never dared to dream of. The boy's mother had written an anonymous letter once, sent through a trusted intermediary: "Thank you, wherever you are. You gave my son his first birthday outside the ICU." I never respond. I never will. But I remember every name. Every recipient. Every cost.

I place the file back, sliding it gently into its slot, and return to the chamber. Six minutes left. I sit on the old metal stool beside the freezer bank, resting my elbows on my knees, letting the cold settle into my bones, a familiar comfort. I should be exhausted, my body screaming for rest. But I'm not. I am calm. Focused. Every time I prepare an organ, I see Lily's face—not the sick one, not the pale, fragile
~~~

girl in a hospital bed—but the vibrant version of her chasing me through the backyard with a plastic sword, laughing so hard she couldn't breathe.

This girl I am helping tonight—she is someone's Lily. And I won't let her die.

The chamber beeps, a sharp, clear tone. Temperature stabilized. Organ ready. I seal it in the sterile travel case, logging the exact time, batch code, and destination. John's clinic will receive it in forty-five minutes. The girl will be in pre-op by the time it arrives. She needs to live.

I cross the basement to retrieve the portable cooler from the utility shelf near the far door, my movements fluid, practiced. That's when I hear it. A creak. Soft. Subtle. But not the building settling. Not the mundane sounds of an old structure.

Someone is here.

I freeze. My heart goes still. My breath, already slow and controlled, deepens imperceptibly. I listen again, every nerve ending alert. Another sound. A slight shift of a foot against concrete, a faint scrape. But I am alone. Or... I am alone.

I reach slowly for the scalpel I always keep beside the chamber, its cool metal familiar in my grip. Not for defense, not truly. For control. I remember the kid, Justin. The raw, desperate terror in his eyes. I hope it won't come to that tonight. Not that I couldn't do it, but right now, my priority is to save the girl.

The single bare bulb above me flickers, casting a dancing shadow. I stare at the doorway, my gaze locked on the empty space. Nothing. No movement. No shadow. But I know the feeling. The distinct, unsettling weight of another presence in my meticulously controlled space.

I swallow once, calmly. This basement has only one way in.

And someone has just used it.

XXIV
Daniel

Call it intuition, or just a detective instinct honed by years of chasing shadows, but I find myself here again, in this forgotten alley, drawn by a thread of cigarette ash and a child's phantom laughter. The alley leads to this underground basement; a place hidden in plain sight. Surprisingly, a faint glow emanates from below. Someone is down here. My gut clenches. Luck, then. The basement air stinks of steel and bleach, a sterile, chemical assault on my senses, but underneath it, something else lurks—something sharp and surgical, like pain with a metallic polish. How did I ever miss this when I first canvassed this alley, searching for any trace of Jessica?

I step down the final stair, letting the heavy door fall shut behind me with a hollow thud that echoes in the sudden silence. He knows I'm here.

My eyes sweep the room, taking in the sterile coolers lining the far wall, their glowing status lights a macabre constellation in the dimness. A worn notebook lies open on a metal table, next to surgical gloves. And then, the freezer, stark and chilling, labeled: AB Negative.

And then him. Standing across the room, eyes locked on mine, a kidney clutched in a sealed transport box. Calm. Not surprised. Not startled.

Just... ready.

"You," I hiss, my eyes flaring, recognizing the man from the café.

He doesn't flinch. His gaze is steady, piercing.

"Daniel." He knows me.

The realization hits me with the force of a physical blow, a surge of surprise and pure, unadulterated anger. His voice is low, steady, eerily composed. Like we're old friends meeting over coffee instead of in a secret lab filled with organs and the ghosts of the missing.

Now that I think about it, I have seen him before. Even before at the café.

"You are a teacher, aren't you?"

He has the nerve to smirk. Asshole.

I take a step forward, then another. My gun remains holstered. Not because I want it to—every fiber of my being screams to draw it, to end this now—but because I want him to suffer first. I want answers.

"Don't run," I say, the words a low growl.

"I wasn't planning to."

"Then drop it."

He doesn't. His grip on the transport box remains firm.

"I want to know why," I demand, my voice raw with unleashed fury. "Why her? Why Jessica?"

He stares at me, and I see something flicker in his eyes—not fear. Something worse. Recognition, with a hint of pity.

"So, you are the husband. Tch tch tch. She didn't tell you?" He says, his voice softer now, almost mournful.

"Tell me what?" My throat tightens.

His expression softens further, a chilling shift, like he's talking to someone already dead, someone beyond saving. "She was hurting, Daniel. You think she smiled because she was happy. She smiled because she didn't want you to worry."

"You're lying," I snarl, the denial a desperate shield.

"She couldn't have children. That killed her," he states, his voice flat, definitive.

My stomach drops, a cold, sickening plunge, but I don't let it show. "I knew that. We talked about starting a family, about adoption. Don't even try to make this about that. That's not a reason to kill her."

"She wasn't living. She was pretending. And you—you were working around the clock, chasing shadows. You weren't there. She supported you, but she felt hollow, empty inside."

"You're lying!" I scream, the word tearing from my lungs.

"I gave her a choice. That she could be useful. To others. She... kind of agreed first, then hesitated later. I can't have that now, can I? "

"No—"

"If I've chosen, there is no going back if they change their minds." He pauses, a ghost of a bitter smile on his lips. "Although, I've got to give it to her. She did fight till the very end."

My body shakes with uncontrolled rage. I don't remember drawing the gun, but it's in my hand now, cold and heavy, pointed right at his chest. But I don't fire. Not yet. The need for answers, for vengeance, is a raw, primal hunger.

Instead, I lunge.

The gun skitters across the concrete floor as I tackle him, my shoulder crashing into his ribs, slamming him against the cold, stainless-steel counter with a metallic clang. The kidney transport box hits the ground, bouncing once, then rolling harmlessly aside. He grunts, fighting back fast—faster than I expect; a brutal efficiency in his movements. A fist cracks into my temple, blinding white pain exploding behind my eyes. I slam my elbow into his gut, hearing the wind rush out of him. He throws a knee; I block. Hook him hard in the jaw.

Blood. Mine or his—I don't know. Don't care.

I grab the back of his coat, the fabric rough beneath my fingers, and slam him into the freezer door so hard it dents with a sickening thud. He grabs a scalpel from the table, its polished blade gleaming, and slashes—the cold steel bites into my forearm, a searing line of pain. I roar, twisting, smashing his wrist against the table until the scalpel clatters to the floor.

We are breathing like animals now, harsh, ragged gasps tearing from our lungs. Both of us bloodied. Both of us boiling with a desperate, primal rage.

"You killed my wife!" I scream; my voice raw, hoarse.

"And you're wasting time!" he roars back, his voice surprisingly strong despite the beating. "There's a girl. A child. If I don't get that kidney to her, she dies."

"I don't care!"

"You should! You're a cop, Daniel. Don't forget what that means!"

I headbutt him, a sudden, brutal crack. He goes down hard, hitting the cold concrete with a dull thud. I press my boot to his chest, pinning him to the floor, my breath ragged.

"You think you're a hero?" I spit, bile rising in my throat. "You're not. You're a grave robber with a god complex."

He groans, blood running from his split lip, then—he laughs. A low, guttural, defiant sound. "You know what's funny?" he whispers, his eyes gleaming with a manic intensity. "You're angrier about how she died than about how she lived."

That does it. That single, cruel truth, twisted and venomous, snaps something inside me. I lose it. I drag him up by the collar, my fists flying, knuckles crunching into bone. One. Two. Three hits. Maybe more. He wheezes, gasping, his body going limp under my assault.

And then, somehow—he smiles. A grim, blood-stained baring of teeth.

"You done?" he rasps, his voice barely a whisper.

I freeze, fists shaking, burning. Because I know what's coming next. He headbutts me, hard, the pain exploding in my skull, a blinding white flash. I stumble back, disoriented, my vision swimming. He is up. Fast. Grabs the kidney transport box from where it lay on the floor. Bolts for the door.

I draw the gun. Aim. I pull the trigger, the roar deafening in the confined space, but he dodges it, a swift movement, and is out the door, sprinting into the night.

"Damn it!" I yell, my voice tearing. I follow.

We are tearing through the rain-slicked streets five minutes later—me in my unmarked car, him in his battered black Civic, its taillights a defiant red blur in the distance. Rain whips against the windshield, blurring the world. I can still taste blood on my tongue, metallic and bitter.

If he's right about the girl, if there is a child dying, helpless in a hospital bed... Every primal part of me screams to catch him, to end this, to exact my vengeance. But the sirens in my head, the duty of a cop, are at war with my instincts. If I stop him now, the girl dies. If I let him go, she lives—and he disappears, a ghost once more.

We cut through the city like bullets, past red lights, through empty intersections, the screech of my tires echoing off wet buildings. My wipers squeal in agony, fighting the deluge. I keep his taillights in view, a beacon of my fractured morality.

We pull into the hospital garage at 2:23 a.m. He jumps out, the cooler cradled in both arms, a lifeline in his hands. I follow, slamming my car door shut, the sound echoing in the concrete cavern. Security guards shout, their voices lost in the storm. It doesn't matter. I burst into the ER after him, a whirlwind of adrenaline and fury. Nurses scatter, startled. A gurney, its wheels squeaking, rolls past, a blur of white sheets.

And then I see it. The girl. Pale. Small. Tubes in her arms, fragile as glass. Her mother sobbing beside her, a figure of profound despair. A nurse, her voice urgent, almost reverent, says, "We got the organ!"

He hands off the cooler, his face a mask of exhaustion and grim determination. The OR doors open, a sliver of bright light, and the girl is rolled inside, into the sterile promise of life.

And I freeze. I can't move. Only ragged breaths tear from my lungs, each one a testament to my internal war.

He turns to me, his face swollen, lip split, one eye half-shut, a grotesque mask of our brawl. But he is standing. He walks past me, a phantom of death and salvation, his steps slow but purposeful. Then he is gone.

And I am left standing there, amidst the chaos of the ER, with the girl's mother clinging to a nurse, whispering desperate prayers to a god who hadn't answered until he showed up.

And for the first time in this whole bloody mess... I don't know who the hell I am anymore.

XXV

Joseph

I'm running on broken ribs and pure, unadulterated adrenaline. My left side screams with every jarring movement, a searing, white-hot flame licking at my flesh. My mouth tastes like a coppery battlefield, a grim testament to the blows I've taken. My pulse pounds against my skull like a desperate prisoner, frantic to escape. But I'm still running.

I bolt out the back entrance of the hospital, the automatic doors hissing shut behind me, and take a sharp left into the grimy alley. Trash bags, overflowing and torn, spill their putrid contents onto the cracked asphalt. Graffiti, crude and defiant, smears the damp brick walls. The air is thick with the scent of rot and stale piss and something worse—the lingering ghost of desperation. It doesn't slow me down. Nothing does. Not yet.

Behind me, I hear him. Daniel. His footsteps are heavier than mine, more deliberate, fuelled by a righteous fury. Like he's not just chasing a man—he's chasing justice. Vengeance. Something holy and terrible, a wrath unleashed. He's not yelling. He's not calling my name. He's just coming. Like a storm front, silent and inevitable.

I take the fire escape, my injured side screaming in protest, climbing two rungs at a time, each pull a fresh agony. The rough metal grates bite into my palms. The rooftop hits my soles hard, a jarring impact. I sprint, my legs burning, leap over a dizzying gap between buildings, landing in a crouch that sends a jolt of pain through my ankle. Something twists, a sharp, sickening pop, but I keep going, ignoring the sudden weakness.

"You're not getting away!" Daniel's voice, raw and guttural, tears through the night, closer than I expected. Damn close.

I duck behind an old, rusted vent shaft, gasping for air, my lungs burning. My hand goes to the small of my back, pulling out the knife I stashed earlier—small, sharp, clean. For protection. For control.

A shadow, impossibly fast, passes over the ledge behind me. I whirl, knife raised, just as he's already mid-air, a dark, determined blur. He tackles me. We go down hard, a sickening crunch of bone and concrete.

I slam into the gravel, sharp stones biting into my back. My head smacks against the concrete with a dull thud, sending a wave of nausea through me. My knife skitters across the rooftop, spinning away into the darkness. He punches. My nose cracks with a sickening pop. Blood sprays, hot and metallic, across my face. I twist, slamming my elbow into his ribs, hearing a grunt of pain. He hits me again, this time in the mouth, a brutal, jarring blow. I knee him off, a desperate, clumsy effort.

We both stumble to our feet, circling each other in the dim, flickering light of the distant city, panting like beasts, raw and primal.

"This ends now," he growls, his voice strained, but resolute.

"Then listen to me—"

"I'm done listening to killers!"

I charge. My body screams, but my will is absolute. He meets me halfway, a blur of motion. We collide like freight trains, a brutal impact that rattles my teeth. His fist slams into my jaw, sending another jolt of pain through my skull. I jab his throat, a precise, calculated strike. He coughs, a strangled, choking sound. I grab his shirt, twisting, and slam him into a large, unyielding vent.

But he's stronger than I anticipated. More focused. He shoves me back, a powerful surge of adrenaline, and tackles me again. I hit the gravel, hard, the impact forcing the wind from my lungs in a single, stunned gasp. He pins me, his weight crushing, his breath hot on my face.

His gun is drawn. Pointed right at my head. Shaking with fury.

And still—I smile. A grim, blood-stained baring of teeth. Because I've already won.

"Do it," I rasp, blood dripping down my chin, warm and salty. "You want justice, right? Pull the trigger."

He hesitates. His finger twitches on the trigger. Then, instead of the gunshot I expect, he slams the butt of the gun against my cheek.

The world spins, a dizzying kaleidoscope of pain and darkness. Black spots bloom behind my eyes, engulfing my vision. But I stay conscious, clinging to the edges of awareness.

He grabs me by the collar, lifts me up to his face, his teeth bared, a primal snarl distorting his features. "Why. Did. You. Kill. Her."

Jessica.

His voice breaks on the last word, a raw, agonizing sound. My breath hitches. Not from the pain, but from the sudden, sharp memory of her, so vivid, so real.

"She wasn't living," I say quietly, my voice barely a whisper, yet clear in the ringing silence.

"Liar."

"She smiled for you. Not for herself."

"Don't—" he cuts me off, his voice desperate.

"She couldn't have children. Even though you were okay with it, she wasn't. It consumed her."

His hands tremble, his grip on my collar faltering. "She felt like she failed you. That she couldn't give you the family you both wanted. And she didn't want to take anything from you. Not your time. Not your sympathy. So, she stayed quiet."

"You're lying," he whispers, the denial a desperate, fragile plea.

"I'm not. I talked to her. She told me she didn't want to live if she couldn't be whole. She just wanted it to mean something."

His breath catches, a strangled sound. And in that silence, that agonizing void, I give him the truth. The brutal, unvarnished truth.

"You think I'm a monster. You think I'm insane. But I didn't pick people at random. I didn't chase the healthy. I didn't butcher families." I lean forward, even as he keeps the gun on me, my eyes locked on his. "I chose the ones who were already gone. The ones screaming for help in ways no one wanted to hear."

"You killed them." His voice is flat, accusatory.

"No. I listened. I heard them when the world covered its ears. You call me a killer? Fine. But I'm also the reason that girl you saw tonight will wake up tomorrow. She will breathe."

He says nothing, his face a mask of conflicting emotions. So, I keep going. Faster. Louder. Each word a hammer blow of truth.

"I gave people a second chance. Not the ones dying slowly in their beds, forgotten by the system, but the ones who wanted to live. Who deserved to live. I gave purpose to the ones who didn't want their death to be meaningless."

"You played God." The words are spat out, laced with contempt.

"Someone had to."

"You think that justifies it?"

"I don't need justification. I need results. And I got them." I meet his eyes. Hold them. My gaze unwavering. "The people who want to die—who write their notes, make their peace—they've already left. Their bodies are still here, but their souls have already gone. And I take what's left and give it to someone clawing for one more breath."

"Who made you the judge?"

"No one. That's the point. No one else would step up. So, I did."

Silence. Heavy. Crushing. The only sound is our ragged breathing and the distant wail of approaching sirens.

Then he pulls the trigger.

Click.

Empty. Just a warning.

Instead, he slams the gun across my face one more time, a brutal, bone-jarring blow. I hit the gravel, coughing blood, my vision swimming. Sirens wail, closer now, a rising crescendo. He doesn't run. Neither do I.

Minutes later, they cuff me. The cold steel bites into my wrists. They read my rights, the familiar litany of legal jargon, and drag me to the car. Daniel doesn't follow. He just stands there, a solitary figure on the rain-slicked rooftop. Covered in blood. Mine. His. Jessica's. His jaw clenched, a muscle twitching. His eyes haunted.

Like maybe, just maybe... He sees it now.

XXVI
Daniel

The news breaks before I even leave the precinct. "Angel of Death Arrested — Secret Organ Vigilante in Custody." The headline, a garish smear of bold, flashing red, consumes the breakroom TV. Beneath it, Joseph's mugshot stares out, blood still crusted on his brow, his lip split. But it is his eyes that hold me captive: a faint, almost smug calm, the same look he'd given me as they hauled him off the rooftop, like he'd already won something I don't understand.

Everyone is talking. Phones buzz with frantic gossip. News anchors, their voices breathless, speculate wildly. Hero? Monster? Martyr? No one can decide. But I can. I saw him. I fought him. I bled because of him. He killed Jessica. So why the hell do I feel like I lost?

All the victim's family and friends finally get the answers, and maybe, a closure.

I stare at the screen longer than I mean to, the faces of my colleagues blurring into a periphery of noise. Jack walks in, catching me zoning out. He sets down his coffee mug with a quiet clink, like he's treading around a live wire.

"You okay?"

No. Not even close. I nod anyway. "Fine."

He doesn't press. Just hands me a folder, its manila surface cool against my hand. "What's this?"

"Compiled testimonies. Patient lists. Recipients. We've confirmed thirty-seven successful transplants linked to the organs he trafficked."

I open it. Faces. Smiles. Some tired, some radiant. Hospital gowns. A four-year-old boy with tubes in his arms, giving a shaky thumbs-up, a miracle in miniature. A teenage girl, her eyes wide with newfound life, hugging her weeping parents. A woman with a wedding band, an oxygen mask still resting on her chest, a symbol of life snatched from the brink. I stare at them, every single one of them alive. Because of him.

My throat tightens, a constriction of conflicting emotions. Jack watches me quietly, his gaze assessing, trying to decide if I'm about to fall apart or explode. "Public's going to split," he says, stating the obvious. "Some people think he's a murderer. Some think he's a saint."

"What do you think?" I ask, my voice barely a whisper.

He shrugs, a weary slump of his shoulders. "I think it doesn't matter what I think. You caught him. You did your job."

But he is wrong. Because this—this doesn't feel like justice. It feels like surgery without anaesthesia. Necessary. But unbearable.

~~~

Two hours later, I sit across from Internal Affairs, the sterile interview room amplifying every creak of the chairs, every rustle of paper. They ask me the official questions, their voices devoid of emotion.

"Did you witness the suspect handling human organs?"

"Yes."
~~~

"Was lethal force required during apprehension?"

"No."

"Did the suspect resist?"

I pause, a long beat of silence, and swallow, the memory of our brutal fight flashing through my mind. "Not in the end."

They ask about the confrontation, details of the chase, the struggle. I omit the worst of it. The blood. The raw, guttural confession Joseph had spat at me. The primal moment I wanted to kill him more than I wanted to save anyone else. I keep it professional, clipped and factual. But inside, something is unravelling. A knot I'd held too long, too tightly, is finally pulling free—and it isn't relief I feel. It is a disorienting confusion. Because I have caught a killer. And it doesn't feel like victory.

~~~

At home, the silence is a tangible thing, pressing in on me. I sit on the edge of the bed Jessica once shared with me, her side still untouched. I haven't moved her pillow. Her slippers are still tucked neatly under the nightstand. The blanket still smells faintly of her, a haunting perfume.

Joseph hadn't lied about her. The revelation has crushed me. It broke her, truly, deeply, that she couldn't have children. But to think I never knew the true depth of her despair, how much she truly felt that specific loss, kills me from within.

She did want to be useful. She did feel like a failure—not because she was, not because she lacked anything, but because the world, with its subtle, insidious pressures, often tells women their worth is tied to children and caretaking and a kind of sacrifice that she couldn't give. She felt like she failed me. Failed us. Which wasn't true. We were enough. She was enough. Just not enough in her own eyes.
~~~

That knowledge breaks something inside me all over again, splintering my grief into a thousand sharper edges.

The next day, Joseph's face is everywhere. Just like he was once renowned, though in a much smaller circle, for his organ-preserving equipment and his scientific advancements. For an elementary school teacher, he'd utterly screwed his occupation, transforming his brilliance into something monstrous. Yet, he doesn't seem to see it that way. He'd poured all his twisted dedication, into this. In a way, he has done exactly what he wanted. So, I guess he did win in the end.

Podcasts dissect his life. Talk shows debate his morality. Social media feeds churn with his methodology, his victims, his chilling rationale. Some people call him a monster with a scalpel. Others call him a genius. A rogue angel. A necessary evil. One influencer, their voice dripping with provocative intent, posts: "He killed the dying to save the living. Isn't that what God does every day?" I throw my phone across the room, the clatter echoing in the quiet apartment.

~~~

The first time I visit the hospital again; I don't tell anyone. I just walk in, blending into the background, another face in the crowded corridors, and make my way to the pediatric ward. The girl he saved is in recovery, a fragile bloom of life. Her mother sits beside her bed, holding her tiny hand, a silent vigil of gratitude. She looks up and sees me, her eyes widening recognition, then overwhelming gratitude.

"You're the detective," she whispers, her voice thick with emotion. "The one who helped... with the kidney."

I nod, unable to speak. She squeezes my hand without asking, a desperate, trusting grip. "Thank you. I don't know
~~~

who gave it to her. But thank you."

And I want to say—it came from a dead person. It came from a killer. But what good would the truth do here? It would only shatter the fragile hope cradled in this woman's hands. So, I just nod again and walk away, the gratitude a heavy cloak on my shoulders.

They let Joseph speak to the press once, from behind bars. Just a few sentences. They cut the audio after twenty seconds, a deliberate act of censorship, but I watch the raw version later. Unedited.

"I didn't kill people," he says, his voice calm, resonant even through the low-quality recording. "I ended waiting lists. I ended suffering. I gave the hopeless a chance." His eyes, direct and piercing, seem to bore through the lens, like he's talking directly to me. "I didn't take life. I redistributed it."

And God help me... a very small part of me believes him.

~~~

I request to sit in on his first court hearing. The judge reads the charges, each word a hammer blow against the silence: multiple counts of homicide, illegal possession and transport of human organs, obstruction of medical law. Joseph doesn't flinch. He doesn't even blink. When asked if he has anything to say, he stands, calm as ever, a chilling composure in the face of ruin.

"I did what the system refused to do," he states, his voice clear and resonant. "And I'd do it again." Gasps echo through the gallery, a wave of shock and outrage. I clench my jaw, because I know he means it.

Later, I am asked to testify. Not in court—not yet. For a medical ethics panel, a sterile, academic discussion of the horrors I have witnessed. They want to know the details. How he selected his victims. How he preserved their organs.
~~~

Whether he had help. I give them the facts, the brutal, unvarnished truth of his methods. But not the why. I don't think I understand the why, even now, not completely. Because Joseph didn't just break the law. He broke me.

Officer Bell finds me one night, standing alone in the evidence room, staring at the board. All the photos still hang there, a grim tapestry of lives lost, and lives saved. Victims. Connections. Jessica, vibrant and smiling, in the very center.

"What are you doing?" he asks, his voice soft.

I don't answer.

"You okay?"

"No."

He nods, understanding etched on his face. "Me neither." We stand there in silence, two cops who have done their jobs and feel like utter failures.

~~~

The next morning, someone leaves a letter on my desk. No name. Just a distinctive, looping handwriting. When I read it, I instantly recognize who it is from.

> *"You think catching me ends this. It doesn't. There are still children waiting for hearts. Women waiting for lungs. Fathers waiting for kidneys. And you—you put the solution in a cage. But I don't hate you for it. I pity you. Because when the next person dies on a waiting list, you'll know what could've been done. And you'll do nothing."*

I crumple the paper in my fist, the thin sheet protesting with a rustle. But the words stay, burned into my mind.

~~~

I visit Jessica's grave. There is no body, but there is a headstone now, a quiet monument to a life unjustly stolen. I kneel beside it, the grass cool and damp against my knees. I run my fingers over the carved letters of her name, the contours of the marble.

"I don't know if he was right," I whisper, the words lost to the wind. "I don't think I want to know."

The wind stirs, a gentle sigh through the willow trees nearby. Somewhere close, a distant bell chimes, a melancholy sound.

"I miss you." I close my eyes, tears finally tracing paths down my face.

"And I'm sorry."

The silence offers no answers, only the enduring ache of her absence.

XXVII

Joseph

The cell is six steps wide, four steps deep. I know because I've paced it enough to carve the pattern into my very muscles. There's a rhythm to it now, a monotonous, ingrained cycle. My body moves like a metronome, even when my mind drifts, soaring far beyond these concrete confines. The floor, a brutal slab of concrete, is perpetually cold beneath my bare feet, a constant reminder of my confinement. The bed creaks, a protesting sigh, every time I shift my weight. The toilet, a porcelain sentinel in the corner, gurgles like it's choking on the weight of its own usefulness, on the endless parade of anonymous prisoners. Everything here is mechanical and grey, meticulously built to strip you of your story, to erase your identity until you are nothing more than a number.

But mine doesn't vanish. It grows. Because even here—even in the cinderblock belly of the justice system—I know that my work, my purpose, is alive. And no cage, however formidable, can touch that.

~~~
~~~

There are letters. They started coming two weeks into my holding period, faint whispers from the outside world. Most were screened, of course. Monitored. Redacted with thick, censorious black ink. But even with the ink hiding names and details, I saw enough. A girl from a hospital bed, her handwriting shaky but clear, wrote: "Whoever you are... I think I'm here because of you. Thank you." A mother's note, tear-stained and crumpled, read: "You saved my son. They say you're a murderer. I don't care. You're an angel." One person—anonymous, their handwriting clumsy and almost childlike—simply said: "Don't stop. Even if they lock you away. What you did matters." They confiscated that one, their black markers obliterating the defiant words. But not before I read it twice, the message burned into my memory.

The guards don't talk to me much. Some of them look at me like I'm a ticking bomb, a dangerous anomaly locked away. Others look like they want to shake my hand, their eyes holding a flicker of understanding, perhaps even admiration. One whispered through the bars the other night, his voice low, conspiratorial: "My niece got a liver last year. They don't know where it came from. Think that was you?" I didn't answer. He didn't need me to. The truth hung in the stale air between us.

They let me have one book. I chose *The Plague* by Camus. There's something extremely comforting about reading existentialism in a place built to erase your identity, to strip you of your free will. The idea that absurdity doesn't negate meaning—that, in fact, it gives it structure, a sharp, defiant edge.

People keep asking me if I regret anything. If I'd do it again. The answer is simple, uncomplicated by doubt: Yes. They think time is punishment. It isn't. Not for someone like me. I've lived in time's shadow since Lily died. Since her heart gave out while I stood in the sterile hallway, clutching a brochure about grief counselling, the meaningless words mocking her fading life. She died on a list. Waiting for someone else's tragedy to become her miracle. That's what they don't understand.

They think I stole from people. I didn't. I used the dying to save the desperate. The ones I took were already halfway gone, their souls having already departed their broken bodies. Some left notes, their final, desperate cries for help, signs no one else wanted to read. Some tried to change their minds in the very end, when death was just one step away, a breath away. But I didn't care. They did think about dying. Doesn't matter if it was just once. They made their choice, and that was it. There was no going back once the path was set.

~~~

Lily visits me in my dreams, vivid and real. Not the sick version—not the pale girl, frail and surrounded by beeping machines and endless IVs. She's laughing. Always laughing. Sometimes chasing Mr. Whiskers, my loyal companion, through sun-dappled fields. Sometimes dancing under starlight, her tiny silhouette twirling against the cosmic canvas. Last night she said, her voice clear as a bell, "You're not done, Jo." I woke up smiling, a wide, genuine grin. They didn't like that. People here aren't supposed to smile.

Daniel hasn't visited. Not that I expected him to. He's probably still staring at his wall of photos, dissecting every detail, every fractured piece of me, wondering which version was the real one. The monster who took Jessica, or the surgeon who saved a girl the same night. The answer is both. That's the part he hates. He wants this to be black and white. Clean. Measurable. A simple equation of good versus
~~~

evil. But nothing about life—or death—is clean.

He beat me bloody on that rooftop, his fists a furious blur of righteous indignation. And still, I got the kidney there in time. The girl lived, her breath a testament to my ruthless efficiency. Jessica's heartbeat in someone else before the transplant record was even flagged, another life saved from the brink of death. So many lives. Alive. Because I refused to let the system fail them.

A reporter tried to send in questions through my lawyer, their words designed to provoke, to condemn.

"Do you believe you're a murderer?"

"Do you feel guilt for the lives you took?"

"Do you think you played God?"

My answers, succinct and unwavering: Yes. No. And someone had to.

My court-appointed psychiatrist, a woman with tired eyes and an endless supply of legal pads, keeps asking about control. "You seem calm," she says, her voice measured. "Don't you feel powerless in here?"

Powerless? I smile, a slow, deliberate curve of my lips. "The lives I saved still walk the world," I tell her, my voice resonating with an unshakeable conviction. "They breathe. They laugh. They love. You can lock up a man, but you can't put purpose in a box." She scribbles something in her notebook, her pen scratching against the paper.

Probably: *Narcissistic delusions. Elevated God complex.*

That's fine. She wouldn't understand. Most people don't.

What I did wasn't just mercy. It was math. Life for life. Breath for breath. A balance, if you will. The world runs on trade—money, time, sacrifice. Why should life, the most precious commodity of all, be any different? I took the ones who didn't want their life anymore. And I gave that life to someone who did. How is that murder? How is that evil?

A boy visited last week; his face pressed against the thick glass of the visitation room. Sixteen. Cheeks still pink with youth, a testament to the life he'd been granted. His eyes, heavy with a profound gratitude, met mine. He didn't say who he was. But I knew. He sat on the other side of the glass, phone to his ear, silent for a full minute before he spoke, his voice hushed.

"You don't know me," he said. "But I think... you knew my donor. Or you were my donor, in a way. I got a heart last year. They said it came from a suicide case. I tried to end things once, too. But I didn't. And now I'm alive." He swallowed hard, his gaze unwavering. "My mom says you're a killer. But I think... I think you're something else." He didn't say goodbye when he left. He didn't have to. His eyes said it all.

Some days, I wonder what it would've been like if I hadn't taken Jessica. If I'd chosen someone else that night, another soul teetering on the precipice of despair. Would Daniel still be chasing shadows, still haunted by an invisible enemy? Would I still be free, continuing my work in the dark? I doubt it. His grief met my purpose like flint meets steel. We both burned. Our collision was inevitable. Even though I enjoyed the little cat-mouse chase, the dangerous game of pursuit, even though I was the one who left those deliberate traces and subtly nudged him to find me, I don't regret it. Maybe deep down, I wanted to be known to the world, to have my truth understood, and this was the only way?

My lawyer tells me I'll likely get life. No parole. The charges are stacked—and airtight. Not that I ever expected mercy. This wasn't about freedom. It was about change.

And that? That is still a question.

~~~
~~~

The transplant lists are under scrutiny now. Hospitals are investigating cases they previously ignored, their complacent protocols being rewritten. Families of anonymous donors are asking new, uncomfortable questions. The ethics boards are scrambling, desperate to redefine the boundaries I shattered. My fingerprints are all over this systemic shift. Even from inside this box, this concrete tomb. I am still moving pieces. Still disrupting complacency. Still forcing people to see.

They took my tools. They took my freedom. But they can't take what I've done. And they never will.

Daniel will come, eventually. He'll want closure. He'll want one last conversation—something to end the story right, to find a neat, final chapter to this messy, bloody saga. And when he does... I'll tell him the truth.

That I never wanted to be a killer. That I was made by a system that let my sister die without even blinking, a system that valued paperwork over human lives. That everything I did was for someone else. Not for glory. Not for redemption. But for Lily. For every child who lies in a bed tonight wondering if tomorrow will be their last. For every parent begging the sky for a miracle that the system would never deliver.

I was that miracle. I still am.

This prison isn't the end. It's the echo. And echoes last. Long after the shouting stops, long after the verdicts are read, the echoes will continue to reverberate, forcing the world to listen.

XXVIII
Daniel

I don't bring a gun. They strip you of your weapons before you step inside anyway, a routine humiliation. But even if they didn't, I wouldn't have. Not today. Today isn't about killing him. It's about listening. Or maybe, it's about looking into the eyes of the man who'd ruined my life and asking him the one question I hadn't let myself say out loud, the one that festers in the quiet moments: Was she really already gone?

The guard buzzes me through three checkpoints, each steel door clanking shut behind me with a heavy finality that makes the air grow thick with unspoken weight. My badge gets me in faster than most, a grim privilege. I don't flinch. I've been in worse places than this. Just not with ghosts rattling in my throat.

Joseph is being held in a private unit—for his protection, they'd said.

"High-profile inmate." As if that makes him a celebrity, a perverse icon. As if the world hadn't already built shrines to him in the form of endless think pieces and YouTube documentaries titled things like *Angel or Butcher?* I don't care what the world calls him. To me, he is just the man who killed people. Who killed my wife.

They bring him in shackled at the wrists and ankles, wearing the standard-issue orange jumpsuit, his face devoid of emotion. But the moment his eyes meet mine, something shifts. Recognition. Not surprise. Like he'd been expecting this moment, this confrontation, all along. Of course he had. The guard leaves, the door locking behind us with a resonant clang. A thick plexiglass divider separates us, a transparent wall between two worlds. We pick up the heavy black phones on either side, the plastic cold against my ear.

"Daniel," he says, his voice as calm, as steady as I remembered.

"Joseph."

He studies me, his gaze unnervingly piercing. "You look tired."

"Because I've been watching interviews of the man who murdered my wife being called a saviour by strangers on the internet," I snap, the words hot with suppressed fury.

"Did she ever tell you?" he asks, his voice softer now.

I clench the phone tighter, my knuckles white. "Tell me what?"

"She said she felt like... a shell. Like a mannequin going through the motions of happiness."

"She smiled every day," I retort, the memory a fresh wound.

"Like I said before, she smiled for you. Not for herself."

My breath catches, a sudden, sharp intake of air. He leans forward, his voice low and steady, almost a murmur against the plastic. "She didn't choose to die, Daniel. But she didn't choose to keep living, either. And when I found her that night, she looked... relieved. Like someone had finally seen her."

Silence stretches between us, heavy and profound. Not the kind that fills time. The kind that breaks it.

"I do admit that I killed her," he continues, the confession chillingly casual. "At the very last minute, she did change her mind. She fought so hard. To live. But I killed her anyway. Because it was too late. You see, to me, thinking about death once is more than enough. It's a choice already made."

I force myself to calm down, clear my throat, the dryness a stark contrast to the bitterness in my mouth. "Why did you bring me here, Joseph? What do you want?"

He smiles faintly, a ghost of an expression. "You brought yourself here."

"Bullshit. You sent me a letter."

"You want to know if I regret it. You want to see weakness. Doubt." He shakes his head slowly, a dismissive gesture. "You won't find it."

"I should hate you," I say, the words a weary admission.

"You do."

I nod. "I should want you dead."

"You do."

I lean forward, my voice dropping, raw with confusion. "But I can't shake the feeling that somewhere in the wreckage of your logic, there's something I almost understand."

His brow arches, a subtle acknowledgment. I exhale, a long, slow breath. "You didn't kill people to hurt them. You killed them because you thought they were already halfway dead."

"I *knew* they were already halfway dead."

"You saw mercy where I see murder."

He nods.

"I caught you," I say, the victory feeling hollow. "But I'm not sure if I beat you."

"You didn't." The way he says it—not with arrogance, but with absolute clarity—stings more than if he'd spat in my face.

I shift the conversation, the questions a desperate attempt to find a different angle. "You cataloged your donors like specimens. I saw Justin's name. He for sure was not suicidal. So, tell me. How many were like Justin? People who weren't suicidal, who didn't ask for it?"

He looks down, his gaze distant, and I see a flicker of something new, something raw in his eyes. "One," he says quietly, his voice devoid of its usual calm. "Just him."

I blink, surprised by the admission.

"I never broke pattern," he goes on, his voice a low monotone. "Not until that night when I saw him sneaking in my lab. He chose the wrong path. I had to." He meets my eyes. There is no pride in his voice now. No smugness. Just a raw kind of grief and sorrow. Like he'd been punishing himself with that memory, too. And somehow, I hate him more for it, hate him for the glimpse of humanity that complicates everything.

"I should've killed you on that roof," I whisper, the words heavy with what-ifs.

"But you didn't."

"You're not special."

"I never said I was."

"You're not God."

"No. But God never answers calls from dying people. I did."

The words hang between us like a knife in the air, sharp and undeniable. I can feel my anger rising again—but it is murky now, tangled with something else. Not forgiveness.

Not understanding. Something harder. Truth.

He breaks the silence. "There's something else."

I narrow my eyes. "What?"

"One of the kidneys I delivered—the last one, to the girl you saw—it didn't just save her life. It triggered a domino in the registry. When she received her transplant, a compatible kidney that had been on hold for her was redirected to someone else."

"So?"

"That someone else," Joseph says slowly, his eyes fixed on mine, "was pregnant."

I blink. He continues, each word a steady drumbeat. "Her child was born healthy two weeks ago."

I stare at him. Two lives. From one. Not because of policy. Not because of a system. Because of him.

"You think that changes what you did?" I ask, my voice flat.

"No," he says. "But it confirms it."

I want to hate him. I want to cling to the certainty of his evil. But what do you do when the villain in your story starts sounding like the author?

I hang up the phone. Stand. He watches me, his gaze unwavering. Doesn't speak. Just nods. As if we'd said everything we needed to say. As if he'd known how this would end from the very beginning.

And suddenly, my hand moves, almost on its own, lifting the phone to my ear, again. He mirrors me. The words are out before I can weigh them, a desperate need for truth.

"I just have two more questions." He nods, wordlessly asking me to continue.

"First, where is the child who received Jessica's heart?"

"She goes to my school. The Elmwood Elementary. Her name is Anna." I don't respond. Instead, I just give him a single tight nod.

"What's the next question?" He asks.

"Just *why*?"

~~~

The walk back through the prison feels heavier. Like every step is layered with a weight I can't throw off. I don't speak to the guard. I don't sign the check-out form. I just push through the final gate, step into the startling sunlight, and blink like someone waking from a fever.

The weight of his words crushes my chest, almost stealing my breath, suffocating me. No child should ever endure what Lily went through.

But Joseph is still a killer. That hasn't changed.

However, now... I don't know what kind of man that makes me.
~~~

XXIX
Joseph

The courtroom smells like disinfectant and cold, polished wood, a stark, sterile scent that does little to mask the lingering tension. It is quiet in that reverent way people become when they're pretending to be civilized in the presence of something monstrous. That would be me. At least, that's how most of them see me, a figure of revulsion and fascination.

The judge, a man whose face is etched with the weariness of too many difficult decisions, begins to read my charges. His voice, though he tries for neutrality, betrays a subtle war within him. Part of him wants to spit the words, to condemn me with every syllable. Part of him, I imagine, wants to whisper them, to somehow soften the harsh pronouncement. He doesn't look me in the eye. No one does, except for one man sitting rigidly in the second row.

Daniel.

He stares straight ahead, arms folded across his chest, jaw tense, eyes unblinking, fixed on me. I wonder if he is still trying to hate me with every fibre of his being, or if the cracks are finally showing in his carefully constructed certainty.

"Joseph Garry," the judge intones, his voice resonating through the hushed room, "you stand convicted on multiple counts of second-degree murder, illegal possession and transport of human organs, violation of national health law, and conspiracy to commit medical fraud."

I don't flinch. This is not a surprise. I have outrun them for as long as I could, but the system, slow and ponderous, has finally caught up.

"Given the nature and scope of your crimes," the judge continues, his voice hardening, "this court sentences you to death, with the punishment to be carried out as prescribed by the law."

The words fall like slow thunder, each syllable a heavy weight pressing down on the silence. People gasp. There are a few who sigh with relief. Some whisper, their hushed tones like rustling leaves. I hear a reporter in the back type furiously, eager to capture this moment of finality. A woman on the aisle dabs at her eyes with a tissue. A man clutches his jaw, his knuckles white, as if he wants to scream.

Good. Let them feel it. Let them remember what it feels like when the system actually moves for once—even if only to cage someone who outpaces its glacial indifference.

The gavel strikes, a sharp, resounding crack that echoes like a bell through the courtroom. I nod once, a calm, almost imperceptible gesture, and stand. I let the guards cuff me, the cold steel biting into my wrists with a familiar snap. No drama. No desperate words. I'd already said everything that needed to be said on that rooftop, in that interview room. My purpose is clear.

~~~
~~~

The holding cell is bright. Too bright. Hospitals and courtrooms always share that feature—the harsh, humming lights that are just loud enough to remind you that nothing here belongs to you. Not your thoughts. Not your body. Not even your silence.

But still, I wait. No regrets. No apologies. Many people are alive because of me, breathing, laughing, living lives they would have otherwise been denied. Lily would've been proud.

She always told me I should do something *weird but important.*

I suppose this counts.

XXX

Daniel

The announcement comes two weeks after the sentencing. It is subtle. Quiet. Not the usual media storm of a high-profile execution. No live feed. No breathless debates on cable news. No ominous countdown clocks flashing on screens. Just a bulletin. Just a name. Just a time.

"Joseph Garry — executed at 5:14 a.m., under state protocol. Witnessed and confirmed."

That is it. The final chapter of a killer.

The media outlets run recycled footage – mugshots, courtroom sketches, blurred video of him being led into custody. Some anchors, their voices dripping with righteous indignation, call him a genius gone rogue. Others spat the word "murderer" like it burns their tongues. One guy on a panel even calls him America's Frankenstein, a bizarre blend of scientific hubris and monstrous creation. But none of them question the execution. They show the official statement, a dry, bureaucratic decree. They flash the prison's security footage: a stretcher being wheeled out of a private chamber, the opaque body bag zipped, guards flanking the gurney. Tight protocol. Clinical. No face shown.

Just a white tag on the toe, black ink on pale skin: J.G.

That's all the public gets. That's all they need. Because the story, to them, is over. Right?

I sit at my desk, eyes fixed on the muted television in the corner of the precinct. The fluorescent lights inside hum quietly, a familiar drone. Outside, the city moves on, its ceaseless rhythm indifferent to the drama of life and death. Someone cracks a joke near the vending machine. Someone else prints a report, the machine's whirring a monotonous backdrop. Life churns. And I just sit there, watching Joseph die for the second time.

But this time, the world believes it.

I am the only one who doesn't look away. Because I know what they don't.

~~~

It started three days after the sentencing. I get a call from someone I haven't spoken to in years—a former prison medic I once helped clear in an abuse case. A man with loyalty in his bones and debts in his silence. He tells me, simply, "There's a window."

I ask, my voice barely a whisper, "What kind of window?"

And he says, his voice flat, devoid of emotion, "A controlled substitution."

At first, I think it is a sick joke, a morbid fantasy. Then he sends the files. There is another inmate. Same height. Same weight class. A close facial structure, enough to pass casual scrutiny. No family. No outside contacts. Convicted serial rapist and killer. Multiple appeals denied. A monster, by any definition. He is scheduled for death row transfer in six months. But quietly, quietly... that date gets moved up. And no one notices. Because no one cares when monsters get scheduled for the grave.
~~~

The plan comes from someone else. Not me. At least not directly. I don't orchestrate it, don't pull the strings. The gears are already in motion by the time I decide whether to lift a finger to stop it. And I don't. Not one.

I meet with the warden once, a private, hushed conversation in his sparsely decorated office. He doesn't ask why I am interested, why a detective would be so intimately involved in such a clandestine matter. He just raises one eyebrow, a silent question, and says, "If this happens... he doesn't come back. Ever."

I nod; my voice steady. "I don't want him back. I just want it clean."

The warden taps a folder on his desk, its contents shrouded in secrecy. "Execution staff's already been chosen. No outsiders. No leak risk."

"And the body?"

"Buried in the state grounds under false registry. Anonymous." No trace. No trail. No second-guessing.

When the day comes, I don't go to the prison. I am offered a seat in the private viewing gallery, as all law enforcement witnesses are. I decline. I watch the news broadcast instead, the official version of events unfolding on a muted screen. And I watch them wheel out that covered body. The face is never shown. The toe tag, even that—just a flash. Enough to be believed. Not enough to question. A solemn voiceover declares: "The body was identified and cremated within hours, per Garry's previously recorded instructions." Another lie. But a useful one.

Jessica's photo sits on my desk, framed in polished silver. The only thing on this earth I'd ever loved enough to break the law for. Joseph killed her. And he's not dead. So why does it feel like this is still right?

I get up, walk to the window. The city stretches out in shades of amber and rain, a living, breathing entity indifferent to the moral compromises made in its name. Headlines scroll across every TV screen in the bars below, illuminated rectangles of flashing texts:

"VIGILANTE SURGEON EXECUTED."

"JOSEPH GARRY CASE CLOSED."

"VICTIMS' FAMILIES SEEK PEACE."

They'll get it. Or they'll pretend to. They'll sleep easier believing the monster is gone, that the threat has been neutralized, permanently. And somewhere far away, the real Joseph will open a new file, his hands moving with practiced precision. He'll wash his hands, sterilize a table, and start again. Under rules this time. Strict ones. No more Jessica or Justin mistakes, no more blurred lines. Just mercy. Just function.

I take one last look at the screen. At the stretcher. At the death the world believed happened. And I nod once. Not for closure. Not for grief. But for balance. Because the system, in its rigid, bureaucratic slowness, doesn't heal people. It just cages them.

But maybe—just maybe—this time, we get something right. In the wrongest way possible.

Joseph

A few hours ago...

Time passes differently in a cell. Seconds stretch into an eternity, each one a slow, agonizing drip. Then suddenly, a full hour is gone, vanished without a trace, and you're not sure how. It's a trick of the mind, a cruel game played by confinement.

A guard arrives, his footsteps echoing in the sterile corridor. But something is off. He doesn't make eye contact, his gaze fixed on some distant point beyond my cell. He doesn't say my name, doesn't utter a single word. Just unlocks the heavy steel door, the clang jarring in the silence, and gestures with his head. "Transfer."

"Already?" I ask, my voice flat, devoid of surprise.

He nods, his eyes flicking toward the ceiling for the briefest, almost imperceptible moment—like he is expecting something. Or someone. I rise, my movements calm, deliberate. Say nothing. Just follow.

They take me through an underground tunnel, its concrete walls damp and cold, a secret passage most people don't know exists. It is the kind used for sensitive transfers, for high-profile criminals, for witnesses or judges under threat. But there is no escort team. Just two silent guards and a single unmarked van. No cuffs. That is the second thing that is wrong. A deep, unsettling wrongness that vibrates in the air.

I sit in the van, the interior sparse and unyielding. They don't speak. Just drive. Through side streets and dead zones with no traffic cameras, a deliberate evasion of the city's watchful eyes. Not toward the federal holding center. Not toward any place I recognize. I don't ask. I just watch, my senses heightened, every detail absorbed.

Ten minutes in, I know. Something is happening. Something I didn't plan, didn't orchestrate. Something I can't plan, can't control. Which is rare. For a moment, a fleeting, sharp edge of panic pricks at me. And then... I don't. Because if this is what I think it is—if this is the kind of twist that fits the brutal irony of my story—then someone has moved a piece on the board. And it isn't me.

~~~

They stop in a covered parking garage, its concrete pillars stained with age, nestled beneath an old government building. One guard gets out, his silhouette dissolving into the shadows. The other, his face impassive, hands me a note. No words. Just coordinates. GPS format. Written in stark blue ink on the back of a court docket, a bureaucratic ghost. I open my mouth to ask, but he is already out, his movements swift and silent. The van doors open from outside, a soft click, and I am staring at an empty garage. No press. No witnesses. No chains.

A black sedan is parked thirty feet ahead, its engine a low, steady hum. Running. No driver in sight. I step out, the cool air a shock against my skin. No one stops me. No one shouts. The van drives away behind me, its taillights disappearing into the gloom.

I walk to the car. The keys are already in the ignition, glinting faintly in the dim light. Inside, on the passenger seat, is a phone. No contacts. Just a single text: "Drive. Don't turn around." No name. But I know the tone. I know the restraint. I know the rage, disguised as duty.

I drive. Through city backroads and rural lanes, through farmland and fog and the intense uncertainty of a new, unexpected freedom. It feels like slipping through a crack in the world—a liminal space between law and purpose, guilt and consequence. No police. No helicopters. Just asphalt and breath, the steady rhythm of the engine, the quiet hum of possibility.

I reach the coordinates two hours later. A house. Small. Hidden deep in the woods, shrouded by ancient trees. Not abandoned. Not quite lived-in either but clearly maintained. Inside: sterile tables, their surfaces gleaming. Locked coolers, their contents a silent promise. Medical-
~~~

grade refrigeration units, humming softly. A generator, a low thrum of power. Everything I need. Everything I once had to steal and scrape for, now handed to me like an unspoken promise.

And in the corner... Mr. Whiskers. Sitting like a king on a folded blanket, his eyes, unblinking and knowing, fixed on me. He meows once, a soft, questioning sound, then blinks, as if to say: Took you long enough.

I find a note on the table, folded neatly. It reads:

"You're not a free man. You're a weapon. I let you go, not because I trust you—but because I know what the world looks like without you."

That is it. No instructions. Just the hum of possibility. And one clear message, etched in the silence of the room: "Keep going. But do it clean."

~~~

That night, I sit at the table, the hum of the refrigerator a familiar comfort. I open a file. New patient. New need. New match. And I know... I'm not free. But I'm alive.

And in the quiet, desolate line between wrong and right—between death and purpose—I still have work to do.

~~~

Epilogue

The cabin sits beneath the hush of pine trees and slow, deliberate snowfall, each flake a whisper on the quiet. No name on the mailbox. No tire tracks on the unplowed road, which cradles it in a silence so thick it feels like time itself forgets to move. Inside, everything hums with a quiet, purposeful life. Medical-grade refrigeration units purr. Steel tables gleam under the soft, diffused light. A laptop lies open to a meticulously organized chart labelled "Recipient AB–3A: Viability Check Complete." To the casual eye, it is just another underground clinic, perhaps run by someone adept at avoiding taxes and regulations.

But to a few people—a very few—it is a war room. And its general is alive.

Joseph slices open the vacuum seal on a sterile kidney pack, the hiss of escaping air barely audible, and places it gently in the cooling chamber. His hands move with unhurried precision, steady despite the immense weight of everything he has done, despite the risk that would snap any other man in half. There is no hesitation in his movements, no tremor of doubt. He is a man restored, repurposed. Reborn in shadow.

The file folder in front of him holds four names. Four patients. All terminal. All waiting, their lives hanging by a thread of hope. Each one scouted, reviewed, verified. Not just for organ compatibility—but for will. For the fierce desire to live. For their unequivocal permission, given in a way that the system refuses to acknowledge. He reads every page, noting every pattern, cross-referencing every hospital record with the anonymous reports slipped under his encrypted door by a courier who never speaks, a silent shadow of complicity.

The rules are stricter now. No errors. No misjudgements. No more mistakes.

Mr. Whiskers, a plump, self-assured shadow, jumps up onto the table and sits near the cooler, curling his tail delicately. Joseph looks over, a soft smile touching his lips. "Still supervising?" The cat blinks, a slow, regal acknowledgment. Joseph returns to the file.

Tomorrow, a man named Jerome Blake arrives—terminal lung fibrosis, pain increasing daily, prognosis: three weeks. No family. No debt. No hope. But a note. Written in stark black ink on yellow paper, tucked into the file: "Let my death matter. Let it save someone else." Joseph folds it carefully and tucks it into his side pocket.

At night, he walks the edge of the pine trees, his coat zipped to the chin, breath fogging in the cold. There are no other homes nearby. No neighbours. No children playing in the snow. Only the quiet. Only the acute peace of knowing no one is watching.

Except one person.

~~~

Across the continent, in a city bathed in the lurid glow of red traffic lights and bureaucratic dusk, Daniel sits at a bar on the outskirts of downtown. He drinks coffee. Black. Quietly. The bartender, a woman with tired eyes, doesn't ask for his name. She knows it is one of those nights for him, nights when he seeks the anonymity of dim lights and distant conversations.

Daniel watches the television screen hanging above the liquor shelves, its muted images flashing. A news story runs: "Organ Transplant Wait Times Drop in Record Shift—Medical Experts Baffled by Anonymous Donor Stream." He says nothing. Finishes his cup, the bitter taste a
~~~

familiar companion. And leaves.

He drives to the edge of the city. To a sprawling, desolate warehouse no one uses anymore, its corrugated metal siding rusted and forgotten. Inside, behind an old steel door marked "Property Seized," is a server. A small machine. Clean. Humming with a low, constant thrum. Inside it: a single live feed. A camera, expertly mounted in the rafters of a cabin buried deep in snow, its lens almost invisible. It shows a man in a lab coat working under warm, inviting light. It shows the cat. It shows the cooling chamber.

Daniel always watches. Silent.

He remembers the day he made the choice. He remembers, as the stretcher wheels out another man, another monster, whose face no one will ever see again. He remembers the way the guards' closed ranks and said nothing, their faces grimly neutral. How the cameras all "malfunctioned" for exactly four minutes, a perfectly orchestrated blind spot. How the body was buried anonymously, swallowed by the earth with no trace. And how Joseph, the ghost in the machine, walks out the other side of the fire, reborn.

Daniel doesn't do it for forgiveness. He doesn't do it for closure. He does it because the system failed. Repeatedly. And the one man who fought it—who cut it open and harvested hope from its dying limbs—was a criminal too valuable to discard.

The phone in the corner of the warehouse, a cheap burner, rings once. A voice on the other end, clipped and professional. "You were right," it says. "The child in Chicago? She made it. The lungs took." Daniel exhales, a slow, shuddering breath of relief he hasn't realized he is holding. He doesn't answer. He just ends the call. And deletes the record, severing the digital link.

~~~

Back in the cabin, Joseph wipes his hands on a sterile cloth. The courier returns in the morning. A new name arrives. A new permission. A new ripple of life spreading outwards. He stands by the window, eyes half-lidded, listening to the snow press gently against the glass, a soft, relentless whisper. And for the first time in months... he lets himself feel proud. Not for what he'd done. But for what it has become. A system outside the system. A mercy machine.

Somewhere, the world thinks he is dead. Somewhere, people still believe that the monster is gone.

But here... Here, the angel of death and life, breathes.

Still. Silent. Unrepentant. Alive.

Later that week, Daniel finds himself, as he often does, parked a few blocks from the Elmwood Elementary school. He doesn't approach. He never does. He just watches. The afternoon sun is warm, glinting off the swings in the playground. Children's laughter drifts on the breeze, a joyful, untainted sound. And then he sees her.

A little girl, no older than ten, with bright, curious eyes and a wild tumble of brown hair. Anna. She is chasing a butterfly, her small hands outstretched, her face alight with pure, unburdened joy. He remembers his fractured conversation with Joseph in the prison, the moment he had asked about the child who had received Jessica's heart. He remembers Joseph's quiet confirmation, a single nod that had ripped him apart and, paradoxically, begun to stitch him back together.

He watches the child, so alive, so full of unadulterated happiness. And in the curve of her smile, in the boundless energy of her movements, he sees a fleeting, almost imperceptible echo of Jessica. Not her face, not her features,
~~~

but the essence of her, the life, the vibrance. A life that, in a twisted, impossible way, continues.

A faint, almost invisible smile touches Daniel's lips, a rare, fragile thing. He closes his eyes for a moment, letting the sound of her laughter wash over him, a bizarre balm to his still-raw grief. He misses Jessica with an ache that will never truly fade. But here, in the sun-dappled playground, watching this child, he feels a strange, great sense of balance.

Not justice, not forgiveness. Just... balance.

He starts his car, the engine a soft rumble. And drives away, leaving the child to her laughter, carrying a piece of Jessica's life, and a fragment of an impossible miracle, within him.

The End.

Joseph
Daniel
HARVEST OF DESPERATION

www.ingramcontent.com/pod-product-compliance
Lightning Source LLC
Chambersburg PA
CBHW031132130726
47988CB00006B/2337